Vladimir Nabokov was born in St Petersburg (now Leningrad) in 1899, the son of a well-known Liberal statesman. When the Bolsheviks seized power the family left Russia and moved first to London, then to Berlin, where Nabokov rejoined them in 1922 after having completed his studies at Trinity College, Cambridge. Between 1923 and 1940 he published novels, short stories, plays, poems and translations in the Russian language and established himself as one of the most outstanding Russian émigré writers. In 1940 he and his wife and son moved to America where he was a lecturer at Wellesley College from 1941 to 1948. He was then Professor of Russian Literature at Cornell University until he retired from teaching in 1959.

Nabokov published his first novel in English, *The Real Life of Sebastian Knight*, in 1941. His other books include *Ada*; *Laughter in the Dark*; *Nabokov's Dozen*; *Pnin*; *Invitation to a Beheading*; *Mary*; *Bend Sinister*; *Glory*; *Pale Fire*; *A Russian Beauty and Other Stories*; *Speak, Memory*; *The Gift*; *The Defense*; *The Eye*; *King, Queen, Knave*; *Strong Opinions*; *Poems and Problems*; *The Waltz Invention*; *Look at the Harlequins!*; *Tyrants Destroyed*; *Details of a Sunset*; and, of course, his best-known novel, *Lolita*, which brought him world-wide fame and was made into a film. Many of his books are published by Penguin. He also published translations of Pushkin and Lermontov, and a study of Gogol. In 1973 he was awarded the American National Medal for Literature. Vladimir Nabokov died in 1977 in Montreux, Switzerland.

In the words of one critic Nabokov is 'one of the most strikingly original novelists to emerge since Proust and Joyce ... Not only did he gain a magnificent command of his second language, English, and develop an extraordinary narrative and descriptive skill, but he brought to his task a visionary insight, a romantic verve and a grasp of human character that seem peculiarly his own.'

Vladimir Nabokov

Transparent Things

Penguin Books

PENGUIN BOOKS

Published by the Penguin Group
Penguin Books Ltd, 27 Wrights Lane, London W8 5TZ, England
Viking Penguin, a division of Penguin Books USA Inc.
375 Hudson Street, New York, New York 10014, USA
Penguin Books Australia Ltd, Ringwood, Victoria, Australia
Penguin Books Canada Ltd, 2801 John Street, Markham, Ontario, Canada L3R 1B4
Penguin Books (NZ) Ltd, 182–190 Wairau Road, Auckland 10, New Zealand

Penguin Books Ltd, Registered Offices: Harmondsworth, Middlesex, England

First published in the USA 1972
Published in Great Britain by Weidenfeld & Nicolson 1973
Published in Penguin Books 1975
10 9 8 7 6 5 4

Printed in England by Clays Ltd, St Ives plc
Set in Linotype Times

To Véra

1

Here's the person I want. Hullo, person! Doesn't hear me.

Perhaps if the future existed, concretely and individually, as something that could be discerned by a better brain, the past would not be so seductive: its demands would be balanced by those of the future. Persons might then straddle the middle stretch of the seesaw when considering this or that object. It might be fun.

But the future has no such reality (as the pictured past and the perceived present possess); the future is but a figure of speech, a specter of thought.

Hullo, person! What's the matter, don't pull me. I'm *not* bothering him. Oh, all right. Hullo, person ... (last time, in a very small voice).

When *we* concentrate on a material object, whatever its situation, the very act of attention may lead to our involuntarily sinking into the history of that object. Novices must learn to skim over matter if they want matter to stay at the exact level of the moment. Transparent things, through which the past shines!

Man-made objects, or natural ones, inert in themselves but much used by careless life (you are thinking, and quite rightly so, of a hillside stone over which a multitude of small animals have scurried in the course of incalculable seasons) are particularly difficult to keep in surface focus: novices fall through the surface, humming happily to themselves, and are soon reveling with childish abandon in the story of this stone, of that heath. I shall explain. A thin veneer of immediate reality is spread over natural and artificial matter, and whoever wishes to remain in the now, with the now, on the now, should please not break its tension film. Otherwise the inexperienced miracle-worker will find himself no longer walking on water but descending upright among staring fish. More in a moment.

2

As the person, Hugh Person (corrupted 'Peterson' and pronounced 'Parson' by some) extricated his angular bulk from the taxi that had brought him to this shoddy mountain resort from Trux, and while his head was still lowered in an opening meant for emerging dwarfs, his eyes went up – not to acknowledge the helpful gesture sketched by the driver who had opened the door for him but to check the aspect of the Ascot Hotel (Ascot!) against an eight-year-old recollection, one fifth of his life, engrained by grief. A dreadful building of gray stone and brown wood, it sported cherry-red shutters (not all of them shut) which by some mnemoptical trick he remembered as apple green. The steps of the porch were flanked with electrified carriage lamps on a pair of iron posts. Down those steps an aproned valet came tripping to take the two bags, and (under one arm) the shoe-box, all of which the driver had alertly removed from the yawning boot. Person pays alert driver.

The unrecognizable hall was no doubt as squalid as it had always been.

At the desk, while signing his name and relinquishing his passport, he asked in French, English, German, and English again if old Kronig, the director whose fat face and false joviality he so clearly recalled, was still around.

The receptionist (blond bun, pretty neck) said no, Monsieur Kronig had left to become manager, imagine, of the Fantastic in Blur (or so it sounded). A grassgreen skyblue postcard depicting reclining clients was produced in illustration or proof. The caption was in three languages and only the German part was idiomatic. The English one read: Lying Lawn – and, as if on purpose, a fraudulent perspective had enlarged the lawn to monstrous proportions.

'He died last year,' added the girl (who *en face* did not resemble Armande one bit), abolishing whatever interest a photochrome of the Majestic in Chur might have presented.

'So there is nobody who might remember me?'

'I regret,' she said with his late wife's habitual intonation.

She also regretted that since he could not tell her *which* room on the third floor he had occupied she, in turn, could not give it to him, especially as the floor was full. Clasping his brow Person said it was in the middle three-hundreds and faced east, the sun welcomed him on his bedside rug, though the room had practically no view. He wanted it very badly, but the law required that records be destroyed when a director, even a former director, did what Kronig had done (suicide being a form of account fakery, one supposed). Her assistant, a handsome young fellow in black, with pustules on chin and throat, took Person up to a fourth-floor room and all the way kept staring with a telly viewer's absorption at the blank bluish wall gliding down, while, on the other hand, the no less rapt mirror in the lift reflected, for a few lucid instants, the gentleman from Massachusetts, who had a long, lean, doleful face with a slightly undershot jaw and a pair of symmetrical folds framing his mouth in what would have been a rugged, horsey, mountain-climbing arrangement had not his melancholy stoop belied every inch of his fantastic majesty.

The window faced east all right but there certainly was a view: namely, a tremendous crater full of excavating machines (silent on Saturday afternoon and all Sunday).

The apple-green-aproned valet brought the two valises and the cardboard box with 'Fit' on its wrapper; after which Person remained alone. He knew the hotel to be antiquated but this was overdoing it. The *belle chambre au quatrième*, although too large for one guest and too cramped for a group, lacked every kind of comfort. He remembered that the lower room where he, a big man of thirty-two, had cried more often and more bitterly than he ever had in his sad childhood, had been ugly too but at least had not been so sprawling and cluttered as his new abode. Its bed was a nightmare. Its 'bathroom' contained a bidet (ample enough to accommodate a circus elephant, sitting) but no bath. The toilet seat refused to stay up. The tap expostulated, letting forth a strong squirt of rusty water before settling down to produce the meek normal stuff — which you do not appreciate sufficiently, which is a flowing mystery, and, yes, yes, which deserves monuments to be erected to it, cool shrines! Upon leaving that ignoble lavatory, Hugh gently closed the door after him but like a stupid pet it whined and immediately followed him into the room. Let us now illustrate our difficulties.

3

In his search for a commode to store his belongings Hugh
Person, a tidy man, noticed that the middle drawer of an
old desk relegated to a dark corner of the room, and supporting there a bulbless and shadeless lamp resembling the
carcass of a broken umbrella, had not been reinserted
properly by the lodger or servant (actually neither) who had
been the last to check if it was empty (nobody had). My
good Hugh tried to woggle it in; at first it refused to budge;
then, in response to the antagony of a chance tug (which
could not help profiting from the cumulative energy of
several jogs) it shot out and spilled a pencil. This he briefly
considered before putting it back.

It was not a hexagonal beauty of Virginia juniper or
African cedar, with the maker's name imprinted in silver
foil, but a very plain, round, technically faceless old pencil
of cheap pine, dyed a dingy lilac. It had been mislaid ten
years ago by a carpenter who had not finished examining,
let alone fixing, the old desk, having gone away for a tool
that he never found. Now comes the act of attention.

In his shop, and long before that at the village school, the
pencil has been worn down to two-thirds of its original
length. The bare wood of its tapered end has darkened to
plumbeous plum, thus merging in tint with the blunt tip of
graphite whose blind gloss alone distinguishes it from the
wood. A knife and a brass sharpener have thoroughly
worked upon it and if it were necessary we could trace the
complicated fate of the shavings, each mauve on one side
and tan on the other when fresh, but now reduced to atoms

of dust whose wide, wide dispersal is panic catching its breath but one should be above it, one gets used to it fairly soon (there are worse terrors). On the whole, it whittled sweetly, being of an old-fashioned make. Going back a number of seasons (not as far, though, as Shakespeare's birth year when pencil lead was discovered) and then picking up the thing's story again in the 'now' direction, we see graphite, ground very fine, being mixed with moist clay by young girls and old men. This mass, this pressed caviar, is placed in a metal cylinder which has a blue eye, a sapphire with a hole drilled in it, and through this the caviar is forced. It issues in one continuous appetizing rodlet (watch for our little friend!), which looks as if it retained the shape of an earthworm's digestive tract (but watch, watch, do not be deflected!). It is now being cut into the lengths required for these particular pencils (we glimpse the cutter, old Elias Borrowdale, and are about to mouse up his forearm on a side trip of inspection but we stop, stop and recoil, in our haste to identify the individual segment). See it baked, see it boiled in fat (here a shot of the fleecy fat-giver being butchered, a shot of the butcher, a shot of the shepherd, a shot of the shepherd's father, a Mexican) and fitted into the wood.

Now let us not lose our precious bit of lead while we prepare the wood. Here's the tree! *This* particular pine! It is cut down. Only the trunk is used, stripped of its bark. We hear the whine of a newly invented power saw, we see logs being dried and planed. Here's the board that will yield the integument of the pencil in the shallow drawer (still not closed). We recognize its presence in the log as we recognized the log in the tree and the tree in the forest and the forest in the world that Jack built. We recognize that presence by something that is perfectly clear to us but nameless, and as impossible to describe as a smile to somebody who has never seen smiling eyes.

Thus the entire little drama, from crystallized carbon and

13

felled pine to this humble implement, to this transparent thing, unfolds in a twinkle. Alas, the solid pencil itself as fingered briefly by Hugh Person still somehow eludes us! But *he* won't, oh no.

4

This was his fourth visit to Switzerland. The first one had been eighteen years before when he had stayed for a few days at Trux with his father. Ten years later, at thirty-two, he had revisited that old lakeside town and had successfully courted a sentimental thrill, half wonder and half remorse, by going to see their hotel. A steep lane and a flight of old stairs led to it from lake level where the local train had brought him to a featureless station. He had retained the hotel's name, Locquet, because it resembled the maiden name of his mother, a French Canadian, whom Person Senior was to survive by less than a year. He also remembered that it was drab and cheap, and abjectly stood next to another, much better hotel, through the *rez-de-chaussée* windows of which you could make out the phantoms of pale tables and underwater waiters. Both hotels had gone now, and in their stead there rose the Banque Bleue, a steely edifice, all polished surfaces, plate glass, and potted plants.

He had slept in a kind of halfhearted alcove, separated by an archway and a clothes tree from his father's bed. Night is always a giant but this one was especially terrible. Hugh had always had his own room at home, he hated this common grave of sleep, he grimly hoped that the promise of separate bedchambers would be kept at subsequent stops of their Swiss tour shimmering ahead in a painted mist. His father, a man of sixty, shorter than Hugh and also pudgier, had aged unappetizingly during his recent widowhood; his things let off a characteristic foresmell, faint but unmistakable, and he grunted and sighed in his sleep, dreaming of large unwieldy blocks of blackness, which had to be sorted out and removed from one's path or over which one had to clamber in agonizing attitudes of debility and despair. We cannot find in the annals of European tours, recommended by the family doctors of retired old parties to allay lone grief, even one trip which achieved that purpose.

Person Senior had always had clumsy hands but of late the way he fumbled for things in the bathwater of space, groping for the transparent soap of evasive matter, or vainly endeavored to tie or untie such parts of manufactured articles as had to be fastened or unfastened, was growing positively comic. Hugh had inherited some of that clumsiness; its present exaggeration annoyed him as a repetitious parody. On the morning of the widower's last day in so-called Switzerland (i.e., very shortly before the event that for him would cause everything to become 'so-called') the old duffer wrestled with the Venetian blind in order to examine the weather, just managed to catch a glimpse of wet pavement before the blind redescended in a rattling avalanche, and decided to take his umbrella. It was badly folded, and he began to improve its condition. At first Hugh watched in disgusted silence, nostrils flaring and twitching. The scorn was unmerited since lots of things exist, from live cells to dead stars, that undergo now and then accidental little mishaps at the not always able or careful hands of anonymous shapers. The black laps flipped over untidily and had to be redone, and by the time the eye of the ribbon was ready for use (a tiny tangible circle between finger and thumb), its button had disappeared among the folds and furrows of space. After watching for a while these inept gropings, Hugh wrenched the umbrella out of his father's hands so abruptly that the old man kept kneading the air for another moment before responding with a gentle apologetic smile to the sudden discourtesy. Still not saying a

16

word, Hugh fiercely folded and buttoned up the umbrella – which, to tell the truth, hardly acquired a better shape than his father would have finally given it.

What were their plans for the day? They would have breakfast in the same place where they had dined on the eve, and would then do some shopping and a lot of sightseeing. A local miracle of nature, the Tara cataract, was painted on the watercloset door in the passage, as well as reproduced in a huge photograph on the wall of the vestibule. Dr Person stopped at the desk to inquire with his habitual fussiness if there was any mail for him (not that he expected any). After a short search a telegram for a Mrs Parson turned up, but nothing for him (save the muffled shock of an incomplete coincidence). A rolled-up measuring tape happened to be lying near his elbow, and he started to wind it around his thick waist, losing the end several times and explaining the while to the somber concierge that he intended to purchase in town a pair of summer trousers and wished to go about it lucidly. That rigmarole was so hateful to Hugh that he started to move toward the exit even before the gray tape had been rewound again.

5

After breakfast they found a suitable-looking shop. *Con-fections. Notre vente triomphale de soldes.* Our windfall triumphantly sold, translated his father, and was corrected by Hugh with tired contempt. A basket with folded shirts stood on an iron tripod outside the window, unprotected from the rain that had now increased. There came a roll of thunder. Let's pop in here, nervously said Dr Person, whose fear of electric storms was yet another source of irritation to his son.

That morning, Irma, a weary and worried shopgirl, hap-pened to be alone in charge of the shabby garment store into which Hugh reluctantly followed his father. Her two co-workers, a married couple, had just been hospitalized after a fire in their little apartment, the boss was away on busi-ness, and more people were dropping in than habitually would on a Thursday. At present she was in the act of helping three elderly women (part of a busload from Lon-don) to make up their minds and at the same time directing another person, a German blonde in black, to a place for passport pictures. Each old woman in turn spread the same flower-patterned dress against her bosom, and Dr Person eagerly translated their cockney cackle into bad French. The girl in mourning came back for a parcel she had for-gotten. More dresses were spread-eagled, more price tags squinted at. Yet another customer entered with two little girls. In between Dr Person asked for a pair of slacks. He was given a few pairs to try on in an adjacent cubicle; and Hugh slipped out of the shop.

He strolled aimlessly, keeping in the shelter of various architectural projections, for it was in vain that the daily paper of that rainy town kept clamoring for arcades to be built in its shopping district. Hugh examined the items in a souvenir store. He found rather fetching the green figurine of a female skier made of a substance he could not identify through the show glass (it was 'alabasterette', imitation aragonite, carved and colored in the Grumbel jail by a homosexual convict, rugged Armand Rave, who had strangled his boyfriend's incestuous sister). And what about that comb in a real-leather etui, what about, what about it – oh, it would get fouled up in no time and it would take an hour of work to remove the grime from between its tight teeth by using one of the smaller blades of that penknife there, bristling in a display of insolent innards. Cute wrist watch, with picture of doggy adorning its face, for only twenty-two francs. Or should one buy (for one's college roommate) that wooden plate with a central white cross surrounded by all twenty-two cantons? Hugh, too, was twenty-two and had always been harrowed by coincident symbols.

A dingdong bell and a blinking red light at the grade crossing announced an impending event: inexorably the slow barrier came down.

Its brown curtain was only half drawn, disclosing the elegant legs, clad in transparent black, of a female seated inside. We are in a terrific hurry to recapture that moment! The curtain of a sidewalk booth with a kind of piano stool, for the short or tall, and a slot machine enabling one to take one's own snapshot for passport or sport. Hugh eyed the legs and then the sign on the booth. The masculine ending and the absence of an acute accent flawed the unintentional pun:

$$3 \text{ P}^{\text{hotos}}_{\text{oses}}$$

As he, still a virgin, imagined those daring attitudes a double event happened: the thunder of a nonstop train crashed by, and magnesium lightning flashed from the booth. The blonde in black, far from being electrocuted, came out closing her handbag. Whatever funeral she had wished to commemorate with the image of fair beauty craped for the occasion, it had nothing to do with a third simultaneous event next door.

One should follow her, it would be a good lesson – follow her instead of going to gape at a waterfall: good lesson for the old man. With an oath and a sigh Hugh retraced his steps, which was once a trim metaphor, and went back to the shop. Irma told neighbors later that she had been sure the gentleman had left with his son for at first she could not make out what the latter was saying despite his fluent French. When she did, she laughed at her stupidity, swiftly led Hugh to the fitting room, and, still laughing heartily, drew the green, not brown, curtain open with what became in retrospect a dramatic gesture. Spatial disarrangement and dislocation have always their droll side, and few things are funnier than three pairs of trousers tangling in a frozen dance on the floor – brown slacks, blue jeans, old pants of gray flannel. Awkward Person Senior had been struggling to push a shod foot through the zigzag of a narrow trouser leg when he felt a roaring redness fill his head. He died before reaching the floor, as if falling from some great height, and now lay on his back, one arm outstretched, umbrella and hat out of reach in the tall looking glass.

6

This Henry Emery Person, our Person's father, might be described as a well-meaning, earnest, dear little man, or as a wretched fraud, depending on the angle of light and the position of the observer. A lot of handwringing goes about in the dark of remorse, in the dungeon of the irreparable. A schoolboy, be he as strong as the Boston strangler – show your hands, Hugh – cannot cope with all his fellows when all keep making cruel remarks about his father. After two or three clumsy fights with the most detestable among them, he had adopted a smarter and meaner attitude of taciturn semiacquiescence which horrified him when he remembered those times; but by a curious twist of conscience the awareness of his own horror comforted him as proving he was not altogether a monster. He now had to do something about a number of recollected unkindnesses of which he had been guilty up to that very day; they were to be as painfully disposed of as had been the dentures and glasses which the authorities left with him in a paper bag. The only kinsman he could turn up, an uncle in Scranton, advised him over the ocean to have the body cremated abroad rather than shipped home; actually, the less recommended course proved to be the easier one in many respects, and mainly because it allowed Hugh to get rid of the dreadful object practically at once.

Everybody was very helpful. One would like in particular to express one's gratitude to Harold Hall, the American consul in Switzerland, who was instrumental in extending all possible assistance to our poor friend.

Of the two thrills young Hugh experienced, one was general, the other specific. The general sense of liberation came first, as a great breeze, ecstatic and clean, blowing away a lot of life's rot. Specifically, he was delighted to discover three thousand dollars in his father's battered, but plump, wallet. Like many a young man of dark genius who feels in a wad of bills all the tangible thickness of immediate delights, he had no practical sense, no ambition to make more money, and no qualms about his future means of subsistence (these proved negligible when it transpired that the cash had been more than a tenth of the actual inheritance). That same day he moved to much finer lodgings in Geneva, had *homard à l'américaine* for dinner, and went to find his first whore in a lane right behind his hotel.

For optical and animal reasons sexual love is less transparent than many other much more complicated things. One knows, however, that in his home town Hugh had courted a thirty-eight-year-old mother and her sixteen-year-old daughter but had been impotent with the first and not audacious enough with the second. We have here a banal case of protracted erotic itch, of lone practice for its habitual satisfaction, and of memorable dreams. The girl he accosted was stumpy but had a lovely, pale, vulgar face with Italian eyes. She took him to one of the better beds in a hideous old roominghouse – to the precise 'number', in fact, where ninety-one, ninety-two, nearly ninety-three years ago a Russian novelist had sojourned on his way to Italy. The bed – a different one, with brass knobs – was made, unmade, covered with a frock coat, made again; upon it stood a half-open green-checkered grip, and the frock coat was thrown over the shoulders of the nightshirted, bare-necked, dark-tousled traveler whom we catch in the act of deciding what to take out of the valise (which he will send by mail coach ahead) and transfer to the knapsack (which he will carry himself across the mountains to

22

the Italian frontier). He expects his friend Kandidatov, the painter, to join him here any moment for the outing, one of those lighthearted hikes that romantics would undertake even during a drizzly spell in August; it rained even more in those uncomfortable times; his boots are still wet from a ten-mile ramble to the nearest casino. They stand outside the door in the attitude of expulsion, and he has wrapped his feet in several layers of German-language newspaper, a language which incidentally he finds easier to read than French. The main problem now is whether to confide to his knapsack or mail in his grip his manuscripts: rough drafts of letters, an unfinished short story in a Russian copybook bound in black cloth, parts of a philosophical essay in a blue cahier acquired in Geneva, and the loose sheets of a rudimentary novel under the provisional title of *Faust in Moscow*. As he sits at that deal table, the very same upon which our Person's whore has plunked her voluminous handbag, there shows through that bag, as it were, the first page of the *Faust* affair with energetic erasures and untidy insertions in purple, black, reptile-green ink. The sight of his handwriting fascinates him; the chaos on the page is to him order, the blots are pictures, the marginal jottings are wings. Instead of sorting his papers, he uncorks his portable ink and moves nearer to the table, pen in hand. But at that minute there comes a joyful banging on the door. The door flies open and closes again.

Hugh Person followed his chance girl down the long steep stairs, and to her favorite street corner where they parted for many years. He had hoped that the girl would keep him till morn – and thus spare him a night at the hotel, with his dead father present in every dark corner of solitude; but when she saw him inclined to stay she misconstrued his plans, brutally said it would take much too long to get such a poor performer back into shape, and ushered him out. It was not a ghost, however, that prevented him from falling asleep, but the stuffiness. He opened wide both casements; they gave on a parking place four floors below; the thin meniscus overhead was too wan to illumine the roofs of the houses descending toward the invisible lake; the light of a garage picked out the steps of desolate stairs leading into a chaos of shadows; it was all very dismal and very distant, and our acrophobic Person felt the pull of gravity inviting him to join the night and his father. He had walked in his sleep many times as a naked boy but familiar surroundings had guarded him, till finally the strange disease had abated. Tonight, on the highest floor of a strange hotel, he lacked all protection. He closed the windows and sat in an armchair till dawn.

7

In the nights of his youth when Hugh had suffered attacks
of somnambulism, he would walk out of his room hugging
a pillow, and wander downstairs. He remembered awakening in odd spots, on the steps leading to the cellar or in a
hall closet among galoshes and storm coats, and while not
overly frightened by those barefoot trips, the boy did not
care 'to behave like a ghost' and begged to be locked up in
his bedroom. This did not work either, as he would
scramble out of the window onto the sloping roof of a gallery leading to the schoolhouse dormitories. The first time
he did it the chill of the slates against his soles roused him,
and he traveled back to his dark nest avoiding chairs and
things rather by ear than otherwise. An old and silly doctor
advised his parents to cover the floor near his bed with wet
towels and place basins with water at strategic points, and
the only result was that having circumvented all obstacles
in his magic sleep, he found himself shivering at the foot of
a chimney with the school cat for companion. Soon after
that sally the spectral fits became rarer; they practically
stopped in his late adolescence. As a penultimate echo
came the strange case of the struggle with a bedside table.
This was when Hugh attended college and lodged with a
fellow student, Jack Moore (no relation), in two rooms of
the newly built Snyder Hall. Jack was awakened in the
middle of the night, after a weary day of cramming, by a
burst of crashing sounds coming from the bed-sitting room.
He went to investigate. Hugh, in his sleep, had imagined
that his bedside table, a little three-legged affair (borrowed

from under the hallway telephone), was executing a furious war dance all by itself, as he had seen a similar article do at a séance when asked if the visiting spirit (Napoleon) missed the springtime sunsets of St Helena. Jack Moore found Hugh energetically leaning from his couch and with both arms embracing and crushing the inoffensive object, in a ludicrous effort to stop its inexistent motion. Books, an ashtray, an alarm clock, a box of cough drops, had all been shaken off, and the tormented wood was emitting snaps and crackles in the idiot's grasp. Jack Moore pried the two apart. Hugh silently turned over and went to sleep.

8

During the ten years that were to elapse between Hugh Person's first and second visits to Switzerland he earned his living in the various dull ways that fall to the lot of brilliant young people who lack any special gift or ambition and get accustomed to applying only a small part of their wits to humdrum or charlatan tasks. What they do with the other, much greater, portion, how and where their real fancies and feelings are housed, is not exactly a mystery – there are no mysteries now – but would entail explications and revelations too sad, too frightful, to face. Only experts, for experts, should probe a mind's misery.

He could multiply eight-digit numbers in his head, and lost that capacity in the course of a few gray diminishing nights during hospitalization with a virus infection at twenty-five. He had published a poem in a college magazine, a long rambling piece that began rather auspiciously:

> Blest are suspension dots ... The sun was setting
> a heavenly example to the lake ...

He was the author of a letter to the London *Times* which was reproduced a few years later in the anthology *To the Editor: Sir*, and a passage of which read:

Anacreon died at eighty-five choked by 'wine's skeleton' (as another Ionian put it), and a gypsy predicted to the chessplayer Alyokhin that he would be killed in Spain by a dead bull.

For seven years after graduating from the university he had been the secretary and anonymous associate of a notorious fraud, the late symbolist Atman, and was wholly responsible for such footnotes as:

The cromlech (associated with mleko, milch, milk) is obviously a symbol of the Great Mother, just as the menhir ('mein Herr') is as obviously masculine.

He had been in the stationery business for another spell and a fountain pen he had promoted bore his name: The Person Pen. But that remained his greatest achievement.

As a sulky person of twenty-nine he joined a great publishing firm, where he worked in various capacities – research assistant, scout, associate editor, copy editor, proofreader, flatterer of our authors. A sullen slave, he was placed at the disposal of Mrs Flankard, an exuberant and pretentious lady with a florid face and octopus eyes whose enormous romance *The Stag* had been accepted for publication on condition that it be drastically revised, ruthlessly cut, and partly rewritten. The rewritten bits, consisting of a few pages here and there, were supposed to bridge the black bleeding gaps of generously deleted matter between the retained chapters. That job had been performed by one of Hugh's colleagues, a pretty ponytail who had since left the firm. As a novelist she possessed even less talent than Mrs Flankard, and Hugh was now cursed with the task of healing not only the wounds she had inflicted but the warts she had left intact. He had tea several times with Mrs Flankard in her charming suburban house decorated almost exclusively with her late husband's oils, early spring in the parlor, summertime in the dining room, all the glory of New England in the library, and winter in the bedchamber. Hugh did not linger in that particular room, for he had the uncanny feeling that Mrs Flankard was planning to be raped beneath Mr Flankard's mauve snowflakes. Like many overripe and still handsome lady artists, she seemed to be quite unaware that a big bust, a wrinkled neck, and the smell of stale femininity on an eau de cologne base might repel a nervous male. He uttered a grunt of relief when 'our' book finally got published.

On the strength of *The Stag*'s commercial success he found himself assigned a more glamorous task. 'Mister R.', as he was called in the office (he had a long German name, in two installments, with a nobiliary particle between castle and crag), wrote English considerably better than he spoke it. On contact with paper it acquired a shapeliness, a richness, an ostensible dash, that caused some of the less demanding reviewers in his adopted country to call him a master stylist.

Mr R. was a touchy, unpleasant, and rude correspondent. Hugh's dealings with him across the ocean – Mr R. lived mostly in Switzerland or France – lacked the hearty glow of the Flankard ordeal; but Mr R., though perhaps not a master of the very first rank, was at least a true artist who fought on his own ground with his own weapons for the right to use an unorthodox punctuation corresponding to singular thought. A paperback edition of one of his earlier works was painlessly steered into production by our accommodating Person; but then began a long wait for the new novel which R. had promised to deliver before the end of that spring. Spring passed without any result – and Hugh flew over to Switzerland for a personal interview with the sluggish author. This was the second of his four European trips.

9

He made Armande's acquaintance in a Swiss railway carriage one dazzling afternoon between Thur and Versex on the eve of his meeting with Mr R. He had boarded a slow train by mistake; she had chosen one that would stop at the small station from which a bus line went up to Witt, where her mother owned a chalet. Armande and Hugh had simultaneously settled in two window seats facing each other on the lake side of the coach. An American family occupied the corresponding four-seat side across the aisle. Hugh unfolded the *Journal de Genève*.

Oh, she was pretty and would have been exquisitely so had her lips been fuller. She had dark eyes, fair hair, a honey-hued skin. Twin dimples of the crescentic type came down her tanned cheeks on the sides of her mournful mouth. She wore a black suit over a frilly blouse. A book lay in her lap under her black-gloved hands. He thought he recognized that flame-and-soot paperback. The mechanism of their first acquaintance was ideally banal.

They exchanged a glance of urbane disapproval as the three American kids began pulling sweaters and pants out of a suitcase in savage search for something stupidly left behind (a heap of comics – by now taken care of, with the used towels, by a brisk hotel maid). One of the two adults, catching Armande's cold eye, responded with a look of good-natured helplessness. The conductor came for the tickets.

Hugh, tilting his head slightly, satisfied himself that he had been right: it was indeed the paperback edition of *Figures in a Golden Window*.

'One of ours,' said Hugh with an indicative nod.

She considered the book in her lap as if seeking in it some explanation of his remark. Her skirt was very short.

'I mean,' he said, 'I work for that particular publisher. For the American publisher of the hard-cover edition. Do you like it?'

She answered in fluent but artificial English that she detested surrealistic novels of the poetic sort. She demanded hard realistic stuff reflecting our age. She liked books about Violence and Oriental Wisdom. Did it get better farther on?

'Well, there's a rather dramatic scene in a Riviera villa, when the little girl, the narrator's daughter –'

'June.'

'Yes. June sets her new dollhouse on fire and the whole villa burns down; but there's not much violence, I'm afraid; it is all rather symbolic, in the grand manner, and, well, curiously tender at the same time, as the blurb says, or at least said, in our first edition. That cover is by the famous Paul Plam.'

She would finish it, of course, no matter how boring, because every task in life should be brought to an end like completing that road above Witt, where they had a house, a chalet de luxe, but had to trudge up to the Drakonita cableway until that new road had been finished. *The Burning Window* or whatever it was called had been given her only the day before, on her twenty-third birthday, by the author's stepdaughter whom he probably –

'Julia.'

Yes. Julia and she had both taught in the winter at a school for foreign young ladies in the Tessin. Julia's stepfather had just divorced her mother whom he had treated in an abominable fashion. What had they taught? Oh, posture, rhythmics – things like that.

Hugh and the new, irresistible person had by now

switched to French, which he spoke at least as well as she did English. Asked to guess her nationality he suggested Danish or Dutch. No, her father's family came from Belgium, he was an architect who got killed last summer while supervising the demolition of a famous hotel in a defunct spa; and her mother was born in Russia, in a very noble milieu, but of course completely ruined by the revolution. Did he like his job? Would he mind pulling that dark blind down a little? The low sun's funeral. Was that a proverb, she queried? No, he had just made it up.

In a diary he kept in fits and starts Hugh wrote that night in Versex:

'Spoke to a girl on the train. Adorable brown naked legs and golden sandals. A schoolboy's insane desire and a romantic tumult never felt previously. Armande Chamar. *La particule aurait juré avec la dernière syllabe de mon prénom.* I believe Byron uses "chamar", meaning "peacock fan", in a very noble Oriental milieu. Charmingly sophisticated, yet marvelously naive. Chalet above Witt built by father. If you find yourself in those *parages*. Wished to know if I liked my job. My job! I replied: "Ask me what I *can* do, not what I *do*, lovely girl, lovely wake of the sun through semitransparent black fabric. I can commit to memory a whole page of the directory in three minutes flat but am incapable of remembering my own telephone number. I can compose patches of poetry as strange and new as you are, or as anything a person may write three hundred years hence, but I have never published one scrap of verse except some juvenile nonsense at college. I have evolved on the playing courts of my father's school a devastating return of service – a cut clinging drive – but am out of breath after one game. Using ink and aquarelle I can paint a lakescape of unsurpassed translucence with all the mountains of paradise reflected therein, but am unable to draw a boat or a bridge or the silhouette of human panic in the blazing windows of a villa by Plam. I have taught French in American schools but have never been able to get rid of my mother's Canadian accent, though I hear it clearly when I whisper French words. *Ouvre ta robe, Déjanire* that I may mount *sur mon bûcher*. I can levitate one inch high and keep it up for ten seconds, but cannot climb an apple tree. I possess a doctor's degree in philosophy, but have no German. I have fallen in love with you but shall do nothing about it. In short I am an all-round genius." By a coincidence worthy of that other genius, his stepdaughter had given her the book she was reading. Julia Moore has no doubt forgotten that I possessed her a couple of years ago. Both mother and daughter are intense travelers. They have visited Cuba and China, and such-like dreary, primitive spots, and speak with fond criticism of the many charming and odd people they made friends with there. *Parlez-moi de son* stepfather. Is he *très fasciste*? Could not understand why I called Mrs R.'s left-wingism a commonplace bourgeois vogue. *Mais au contraire*, she and her daughter adore radicals! Well, I said, Mr R., *lui*, is immune to politics. My darling thought that was the trouble with him. Toffee-cream neck with a tiny gold cross and a *grain de beauté*. Slender, athletic, lethal!'

10

He did do something about it, despite all that fond criticism of himself. He wrote her a note from the venerable Versex Palace where he was to have cocktails in a few minutes with our most valuable author whose best book you did not like. Would you permit me to call on you, say Wednesday, the fourth? Because I shall be by then at the Ascot Hotel in your Witt, where I am told there is some excellent skiing even in summer. The main object of my stay *here*, on the other hand, is to find out when the old rascal's current book will be finished. It is queer to recall how keenly only the day before yesterday I had looked forward to seeing the great man at last in the flesh.

There was even more of it than our Person had expected on the strength of recent pictures. As he peeped through a vestibule window and watched him emerge from his car, no clarion of repute, no scream of glamour reverbed through his nervous system, which was wholly occupied with the bare-thighed girl in the sun-shot train. Yet what a grand sight R. presented – his handsome chauffeur helping the obese old boy on one side, his black-bearded secretary supporting him on the other, and two *chasseurs* from the hotel going through a mimicry of tentative assistance on the porch steps. The reporter in Person noted that Mr R. wore Wallabees of a velvety cocoa shade, a lemon shirt with a lilac neck scarf, and a rumpled gray suit that seemed to have no distinction whatever – at least, to a plain American. Hullo, Person! They sat down in the lounge near the bar.

The illusory quality of the entire event was enhanced by

the appearance and speech of the two characters. That monumental man with his clayey makeup and false grin, and Mr Tamworth of the brigand's beard, seemed to be acting out a stiffly written scene for the benefit of an invisible audience from which Person, a dummy, kept turning away as if moved with his chair by Sherlock's concealed landlady, no matter how he sat or where he looked in the course of the brief but boozy interview. It was indeed all sham and waxworks as compared to the reality of Armande, whose image was stamped on the eye of his mind and shone through the show at various levels, sometimes upside down, sometimes on the teasing marge of his field of vision, but always there, always, true and thrilling. The commonplaces he and she had exchanged blazed with authenticity when placed for display against the forced guffaws in the bogus bar.

'Well, you certainly look remarkably fit,' said Hugh with effusive mendacity after the drinks had been ordered.

Baron R. had coarse features, a sallow complexion, a lumpy nose with enlarged pores, shaggy bellicose eyebrows, an unerring stare, and a bulldog mouth full of bad teeth. The streak of nasty inventiveness so conspicuous in his writings also appeared in the prepared parts of his speech, as when he said, as he did now, that far from 'looking fit' he felt more and more a creeping resemblance to the cinema star Reubenson who once played old gangsters in Florida-staged films; but no such actor existed.

'Anyway – how are you?' asked Hugh, pressing his disadvantage.

'To make a story quite short,' replied Mr R. (who had an exasperating way not only of trotting out hackneyed formulas in his would-be colloquial thickly accented English, but also of getting them wrong), 'I had not been feeling any too healthy, you know, during the winter. My liver, you know, was holding something against me.'

He took a long sip of whiskey, and, rinsing his mouth with it in a manner Person had never yet witnessed, very slowly replaced his glass on the low table. Then, *à deux* with the muzzled stuff, he swallowed it and shifted to his second English style, the grand one of his most memorable characters:

'Insomnia and her sister Nocturia harry me, of course, but otherwise I am as hale as a pane of stamps. I don't think you met Mr Tamworth. Person, pronounced Parson; and Tamworth: like the English breed of black-blotched swine.'

'No,' said Hugh, 'it does not come from Parson, but rather from Peterson.'

'O.K., son. And how's Phil?'

They discussed briefly R.'s publisher's vigor, charm, and acumen.

'Except that he wants me to write the wrong books. He wants –' assuming a coy throaty voice as he named the titles of a competitor's novels, also published by Phil – 'he wants *A Boy for Pleasure* but would settle for *The Slender Slut,* and all *I* can offer him is not *Tralala* but the first and dullest tome of my *Tralatitions.*'

'I assure you that he is waiting for the manuscript with utmost impatience. By the way –'

By the way, indeed! There ought to exist some rhetorical term for that twist of nonlogic. A unique view through a black weave ran by the way. By the way, I shall lose my mind if I do not get her.

'– by the way, I met a person yesterday who has just seen your stepdaughter –'

'Former stepdaughter,' corrected Mr R. 'Quite a time no see, and I hope it remains so. Same stuff, son' (this to the barman).

'The occasion was rather remarkable. Here was this young woman, reading –'

'Excuse me,' said the secretary warmly, and folding a note he had just scribbled, passed it to Hugh.

'Mr R. resents all mention of Miss Moore and her mother.'

And I don't blame him. But where was Hugh's famous tact? Giddy Hugh knew quite well the whole situation, having got it from Phil, not Julia, an impure but reticent little girl.

This part of our translucing is pretty boring, yet we must complete our report.

Mr R. had discovered one day, with the help of a hired follower, that his wife Marion was having an affair with Christian Pines, son of the well-known cinema man who had directed the film *Golden Windows* (precariously based on the best of our author's novels). Mr R. welcomed the situation since he was assiduously courting Julia Moore, his eighteen-year-old stepdaughter, and now had plans for the future, well worthy of a sentimental lecher whom three or four marriages had not sated yet. Very soon, however, he learned from the same sleuth, who is at present dying in a hot dirty hospital on Formosa, an island, that young Pines, a handsome frog-faced playboy, soon also to die, was the lover of both mother and daughter, whom he had serviced in Cavaliere, Cal., during two summers. Hence the separation acquired more pain and plenitude than R. had expected. In the midst of all this, our Person, in his discreet little way (though actually he was half an inch taller than big R.), had happened to nibble, too, at the corner of the crowded canvas.

Julia liked tall men with strong hands and sad eyes. Hugh had met her first at a party in a New York house. A couple of days later he ran into her at Phil's place and she asked if he cared to see *Cunning Stunts*, an 'avant garde' hit, she had two tickets for herself and her mother, but the latter had had to leave for Washington on legal business (related to the divorce proceedings as Hugh correctly surmised): would he care to escort her? In matters of art, 'avant garde' means little more than conforming to some daring philistine fashion, so, when the curtain opened, Hugh was not surprised to be regaled with the sight of a naked hermit sitting on a cracked toilet in the middle of an empty stage. Julia giggled, preparing for a delectable evening. Hugh was moved to enfold in his shy paw the childish hand that had accidentally touched his kneecap. She was wonderfully pleasing to the sexual eye with her doll's face, her slanting eyes and topaz-teared earlobes, her slight form in an orange blouse and black skirt, her slender-jointed limbs, her exotically sleek hair squarely cut on the forehead. No less pleasing was the conjecture that in his Swiss retreat, Mr R., who had bragged to an interviewer of being blessed with a goodish amount of telepathic power, was bound to experience a twinge of jealousy at the present moment of spacetime.

Rumours had been circulating that the play might be banned after its very first night. A number of rowdy young demonstrators in protest against that contingency managed to disrupt the performance which they were actually supporting. The bursting of a few festive little bombs filled the hall with bitter smoke, a brisk fire started among unwound serpentines of pink and green toilet paper, and the theater was evacuated. Julia announced she was dying of frustration and thirst. A famous bar next to the theater proved hopelessly crowded and 'in the radiance of an Edenic simplification of mores' (as R. wrote in another connection) our Person took the girl to his flat. Unwisely he wondered – after a too passionate kiss in the taxi had led him to spill a few firedrops of impatience – if he would not disappoint the expectations of Julia, who according to Phil had been debauched at thirteen by R., right at the start of her mother's disastrous marriage.

The bachelor's flat Hugh rented on East Sixty-fifth had been found for him by his firm. Now it so happened that those rooms were the same in which Julia had visited one of her best young males a couple of years before. She had the good taste to say nothing, but the image of that youth, whose death in a remote war had affected her greatly, kept coming out of the bathroom or fussing with things in the fridge, and interfering so oddly with the small business in hand that she refused to be unzipped and bedded. Naturally after a decent interval the child gave in and soon found herself assisting big Hugh in his blundersome lovemaking. No sooner, however, had the poking and panting run their customary course and Hugh, with a rather forlorn show of jauntiness, had gone for more drinks, than the image of bronzed and white-buttocked Jimmy Major again replaced bony reality. She noticed that the closet mirror as seen from the bed reflected exactly the same still-life arrangement, oranges in a wooden bowl, as it had in the garland-brief days of Jim, a voracious consumer of the centenarian's fruit. She was almost sorry when upon looking around she located the source of the vision in the folds of her bright things thrown over the back of a chair.

She canceled their next assignation at the last moment and soon afterward went off to Europe. In Person's mind the affair left hardly anything more than a stain of light lipstick on tissue paper — and a romantic sense of having embraced a great writer's sweetheart. Time, however, sets to work on those ephemeral affairs, and a new flavor is added to the recollection.

We now see a torn piece of *La Stampa* and an empty wine bottle. A lot of construction work was going on.

12

A lot of construction work was going on around Witt, scarring and muddying the entire hillside upon which he was told he would find Villa Nastia. Its immediate surroundings had more or less been tidied up, forming an oasis of quiet amidst the clanging and knocking wilderness of clay and cranes. There even gleamed a boutique among the shops forming a hemicircle around a freshly planted young rowan under which some litter had already been left, such as a workman's empty bottle and an Italian newspaper. Person's power of orientation now failed him but a woman selling apples from a neighboring stall set him straight again. An overaffectionate large white dog started to frisk unpleasantly in his wake and was called back by the woman.

He walked up a steepish asphalted path which had a white wall on one side with firs and larches showing above. A grilled door in it led to some camp or school. The cries of children at play came from behind the wall and a shuttlecock sailed over it to land at his feet. He ignored it, not being the sort of man who picks up things for strangers – a glove, a rolling coin.

A little farther, an interval in the stone wall revealed a short flight of stairs and the door of a whitewashed bungalow signed Villa Nastia in French cursive. As happens so often in R.'s fiction, 'nobody answered the bell'. Hugh noticed several other steps lateral to the porch, descending (after all that stupid climbing!) into the pungent dampness of boxwood. These led him around the house and into its garden. A boarded, only half-completed splash pool adjoined a small lawn, in the center of which a stout middle-aged lady, with greased limbs of a painful pink, lay sun-bathing in a deck chair. A copy, no doubt the same, of the *Figures* et cetera paperback, with a folded letter (which we thought wiser our Person should not recognize) acting as marker, lay on top of the one-piece swimsuit into which her main bulk had been stuffed.

Madame Charles Chamar, *née* Anastasia Petrovna Pota-pov (a perfectly respectable name that her late husband garbled as 'Patapouf'), was the daughter of a wealthy cattle dealer who had emigrated with his family to England from Ryazan via Kharbin and Ceylon soon after the Bolshevist revolution. She had long grown accustomed to entertaining this or that young man whom capricious Armande had stood up; but the new beau was dressed like a salesman, and had something about him (your genius, Person!) that puzzled and annoyed Madame Chamar. She liked people to fit. The Swiss boy, with whom Armande was skiing at the moment on the permanent snows high above Witt, fitted. So did the Blake twins. So did the old guide's son, golden-haired Jacques, a bobsled champion. But my gangly and gloomy Hugh Person, with his awful tie, vulgarly fastened to his cheap white shirt, and impossible chestnut suit, did not belong to her accepted world. When told that Armande was enjoying herself elsewhere and might not be back for tea, he did not bother to conceal his surprise and displeas-ure. He stood scratching his cheek. The inside of his Tyro-lean hat was dark with sweat. Had Armande got his letter?

Madame Chamar answered in the noncommittal nega-tive – though she might have consulted the telltale book marker, but out of a mother's instinctive prudence refrained from doing so. Instead she popped the paperback into her garden bag. Automatically, Hugh mentioned that he had recently visited its author.

'He lives somewhere in Switzerland, I think?'

'Yes, at Diablonnet, near Versex.'

'Diablonnet always reminds me of the Russian for "apple trees": *yabloni*. He has a nice house?'

'Well, we met in Versex, in a hotel, not at his home. I'm told it's a very large and a very old-fashioned place. We discussed business matters. Of course the house is always full of his rather, well, frivolous guests. I shall wait for a little while and then go.'

He refused to shed his jacket and relax in a lawn chair alongside Madame Chamar. Too much sun caused his head to swim, he explained. '*Alors allons dans la maison,*' she said, faithfully translating from Russian. Seeing the efforts she was making to rise, Hugh offered to help her; but Madame Chamar bade him sharply stand well away from her chair lest his proximity prove a 'psychological obstruction'. Her unwieldy corpulence could be moved only by means of one precise little wiggle; in order to make it she had to concentrate upon the idea of trying to fool gravity until something clicked inwardly and the right jerk happened like the miracle of a sneeze. Meantime she lay in her chair motionless, and as it were ambushed, with brave sweat glistening on her chest and above the purple arches of her pastel eyebrows.

'This is completely unnecessary,' said Hugh, 'I am quite happy to wait here in the shade of a tree, but shade I must have. I never thought it would be so hot in the mountains.'

Abruptly, Madame Chamar's entire body gave such a start that the frame of her deck chair emitted an almost human cry. The next moment she was in a sitting position, with both feet on the ground.

'Everything is well,' she declared cozily, and stood up, now robed in bright terry cloth with the suddenness of a magic metamorphosis. 'Come, I want to offer you a nice cold drink and show you my albums.'

The drink turned out to be a tall faceted glass of tepid tapwater with a spoonful of homemade strawberry jam clouding it a mallowish hue. The albums, four big bound volumes, were laid out on a very low, very round table in the very *moderne* living room.

'I now leave you for some minutes,' said Madame Chamar, and in full view of the public ascended with ponderous energy the completely visible and audible stairs leading to a similarly overt second floor, where one could see a bed through an open door and a bidet through another. Armande used to say that this product of her late father's art was a regular showpiece attracting tourists from distant countries such as Rhodesia and Japan.

The albums were quite as candid as the house, though less depressing. The Armande series, which exclusively interested our *voyeur malgré lui*, was inaugurated by a photograph of the late Potapov, in his seventies, looking very dapper with his gray little imperial and his Chinese house jacket, making the wee myopic sign of the Russian cross over an invisible baby in its deep cot. Not only did the snapshots follow Armande through all the phases of the past and all the improvements of amateur photography, but the girl also came in various states of innocent undress. Her parents and aunts, the insatiable takers of cute pictures, believed in fact that a girl child of ten, the dream of a Lutwidgean, had the same right to total nudity as an infant. The visitor constructed a pile of albums to screen the flame of his interest from anybody overheard on the landing, and returned several times to the pictures of little Armande in her bath, pressing a proboscidate rubber toy to her shiny stomach or standing up, dimple-bottomed, to be lathered. Another revelation of impuberal softness (its middle line just distinguishable from the less vertical grass-blade next to it) was afforded by a photo of her in which she sat in the buff on the grass, combing her sun-shot hair and spreading wide, in false perspective, the lovely legs of a giantess.

He heard a toilet flush upstairs and with a guilty wince slapped the thick book shut. His retractile heart moodily withdrew, its throbs quietened; but nobody came down from those infernal heights, and he went back, rumbling, to his silly pictures.

Toward the end of the second album the photography burst into color to celebrate the vivid vestiture of her adolescent molts. She appeared in floral frocks, fancy slacks, tennis shorts, swimsuits, amidst the harsh greens and blues of the commercial spectrum. He discovered the elegant angularity of her sun-tanned shoulders, the long line of her haunch. He learned that at eighteen the torrent of her pale hair reached the small of her back. No matrimonial agency could have offered its clients such variations on the theme of one virgin. In the third album he found, with an enjoyable sense of homecoming, glimpses of his immediate surroundings: the lemon and black cushions of the divan at the other end of the room and the Denton mount of a birdwing butterfly on the mantelpiece. The fourth, incomplete album began with a sparkle of her chastest images: Armande in a pink parka, Armande jewel-bright, Armande careening on skis through the sugar dust.

At last, from the upper part of the transparent house, Madame Chamar warily trudged downstairs, the jelly of a bare forearm wobbling as she clutched at the balustrade rail. She was now clad in an elaborate summer dress with flounces, as if she too, like her daughter, had been passing through several stages of change. 'Don't get up, don't get up,' she cried, patting the air with one hand, but Hugh insisted he'd better go. 'Tell her,' he added, 'tell your daughter when she returns from her glacier, that I was extremely disappointed. Tell her I shall be staying a week, two weeks, three weeks here, at the grim Ascot Hotel in the pitiful

45

village of Witt. Tell her I shall telephone if she does not. Tell her,' he continued, now walking down a slippery path among cranes and power shovels immobilized in the gold of the late afternoon, 'tell her that my system is poisoned by her, by her twenty sisters, her twenty dwindlings in backcast, and that I shall perish if I cannot have her.'

He was still rather simple as lovers go. One might have said to fat, vulgar Madame Chamar: how dare you exhibit your child to sensitive strangers? But our Person vaguely imagined that this was a case of modern immodesty current in Madame Chamar's set. What 'set', good Lord? The lady's mother had been a country veterinary's daughter, same as Hugh's mother (by the only coincidence worth noting in the whole rather sad affair). Take those pictures away, you stupid nudist!

She rang him up around midnight, waking him in the pit of an evanescent, but definitely bad, dream (after all that melted cheese and young potatoes with a bottle of green wine at the hotel's *carnotzet*). As he scrabbled up the receiver, he groped with the other hand for his reading glasses, without which, by some vagary of concomitant senses, he could not attend to the telephone properly.

'You Person?' asked her voice.

He already knew, ever since she had recited the contents of the card he had given her on the train, that she pronounced his first name as 'You'.

'Yes, it's me, I mean "you". I mean you mispronounce it most enchantingly.'

'I do not mispronounce anything. Look, I never received –'

'Oh, you do! You drop your haitches like – like pearls into a blindman's cup.'

'Well, the correct pronunciation is "cap". I win. Now listen, tomorrow I'm occupied, but what about Friday – if you can be ready *à sept heures précises*?'

He certainly could.

She invited 'Percy', as she declared she would call him
from now on, since he detested 'Hugh', to come with her for
a bit of summer skiing at Drakonita, or Darkened Heat, as
he misheard it, which caused him to conjure up a dense
forest protecting romantic ramblers from the blue blaze of
an alpine noon. He said he had never learned to ski on a
holiday at Sugarwood, Vermont, but would be happy to
stroll beside her, along a footpath not only provided for
him by fancy but also swept clean with a snowman's
broom – one of those instant unverified visions which can
fool the cleverest man.

13

Now we have to bring into focus the main street of Witt as it was on Thursday, the day after her telephone call. It teems with transparent people and processes, into which and through which we might sink with an angel's or author's delight, but we have to single out for this report only one Person. Not an extensive hiker, he limited his loafing to a tedious survey of the village. A grim stream of cars rolled and rolled, some seeking with the unwieldy wariness of reluctant machinery a place to park, others coming from, or heading for, the much more fashionable resort of Thur, twenty miles north. He passed several times by the old fountain dribbling through the geranium-lined trough of a hollowed log; he examined the post office and the bank, the church and the tourist agency, and a famous black hovel that was still allowed to survive with its cabbage patch and scarecrow crucifix between a boarding-house and a laundry.

He drank beer in two different taverns. He lingered before a sports shop; relingered – and bought a nice gray turtleneck sweater with a tiny and very pretty American flag embroidered over the heart. 'Made in Turkey', whispered its label.

He decided it was time for some more refreshments – and saw her sitting at a sidewalk café. You swerved toward her, thinking she was alone; then noticed, too late, a second handbag on the opposite chair. Simultaneously her companion came out of the tea shop and, resuming her seat, said in that lovely New York voice, with that harlot dash he would have recognized even in heaven:

'The john is a joke.'

Meanwhile Hugh Person, unable to shed the mask of an affable grin, had come up and was invited to join them.

An adjacent customer, comically resembling Person's late Aunt Melissa whom we like very much, was reading l'*Erald Tribune*. Armande believed (in the vulgar connotation of the word) that Julia Moore had met Percy. Julia believed she had. So did Hugh, indeed, yes. Did his aunt's double permit him to borrow her spare chair? He was welcome to it. She was a dear soul, with five cats, living in a toy house, at the end of a birch avenue, in the quietest part of –

Interrupting us with an earsplitting crash an impassive waitress, a poor woman in her own right, dropped a tray with lemonades and cakes, and crouched, splitting into many small quick gestures peculiar to that woman, her face impassive.

Armande informed Percy that Julia had come all the way from Geneva to consult her about the translation of a number of phrases with which she, Julia, who was going tomorrow to Moscow, desired to 'impress' her Russian friends. Percy, here, worked for her stepfather.

'My *former* stepfather, thank Heavens,' said Julia. 'By the way, Percy, if that's your *nom de voyage*, perhaps you may help. As she explained, I want to dazzle some people in Moscow, who promised me the company of a famous young Russian poet. Armande has supplied me with a number of darling words, but we got stuck at –' (taking a slip of paper from her bag) – 'I want to know how to say: "What a cute little church, what a big snowdrift." You see we do it first into French and she thinks "snowdrift" is *rafale de neige*, but I'm sure it can't be *rafale* in French and *rafalovich* in Russian, or whatever they call a snowstorm.'

'The word you want,' said our Person, 'is *congère*, feminine gender, I learned it from my mother.'

'Then it's *sugrob* in Russian,' said Armande and added dryly: 'Only there won't be much snow there in August.'

Julia laughed. Julia looked happy and healthy. Julia had grown even prettier than she had been two years ago. Shall I now see her in dreams with those new eyebrows, that new long hair? How fast do dreams catch up with new fashions? Will the next dream still stick to her Japanese-doll hairdo?

'Let me order something for you,' said Armande to Percy, not making, however, the offering gesture that usually goes with that phrase.

Percy thought he would like a cup of hot chocolate. The dreadful fascination of meeting an old flame in public! Armande had nothing to fear, naturally. *She* was in a totally different class, beyond competition. Hugh recalled R.'s famous novella *Three Tenses*.

'There was something else we didn't quite settle, Armande, or did we?'

'Well, we spent two hours at it,' remarked Armande, rather grumpily – not realizing, perhaps, that she had nothing to fear. The fascination was of a totally different, purely intellectual or artistic order, as brought out so well in *Three Tenses*: a fashionable man in a night-blue tuxedo is supping on a lighted veranda with three bare-shouldered beauties, Alice, Beata, and Claire, who have never seen one another before. A. is a former love, B. is his present mistress, C. is his future wife.

He regretted now not having coffee as Armande and Julia were having. The chocolate proved unpalatable. You were served a cup of hot milk. You also got, separately, a little sugar and a dainty-looking envelope of sorts. You ripped open the upper margin of the envelope. You added the beige dust it contained to the ruthlessly homogenized milk in your cup. You took a sip – and hurried to add sugar. But no sugar could improve the insipid, sad, dishonest taste.

Armande, who had been following the various phases of his astonishment and disbelief, smiled and said:

'Now you know what "hot chocolate" has come to in Switzerland. My mother,' she continued, turning to Julia (who with the revelatory *sans-gêne* of the Past Tense, though actually she prided herself on her reticence, had lunged with her little spoon toward Hugh's cup and collected a sample), 'my mother actually broke into tears when she was first served this stuff, because she remembered so tenderly the chocolate of her chocolate childhood.'

'Pretty beastly,' agreed Julia, licking her plump pale lips, 'but still I prefer it to our American fudge.'

'That's because you are the most unpatriotic creature in the world,' said Armande.

The charm of the Past Tense lay in its secrecy. Knowing Julia, he was quite sure she would not have told a chance friend about their affair – one sip among dozens of swallows. Thus, at this precious and brittle instant, Julia and he (*alias* Alice and the narrator) formed a pact of the past, an impalpable pact directed against reality as represented by the voluble street corner, with its swish-passing automobiles, and trees, and strangers. The B. of the trio was Busy Witt, while the main stranger – and this touched off another thrill – was his sweetheart of the morrow, Armande, and Armande was as little aware of the future (which the author, of course, knew in every detail) as she was of the past that Hugh now retasted with his brown-dusted milk. Hugh, a sentimental simpleton, and somehow not a very *good* Person (good ones are above that, he was merely a rather dear one), was sorry that no music accompanied the scene, no Rumanian fiddler dipped heartward for two monogram-entangled sakes. There was not even a mechanical rendition of 'Fascination' (a waltz) by the café's loudplayer. Still there did exist a kind of supporting rhythm formed by the voices of foot passengers, the clink of crockery, the mountain wind in the venerable mass of the corner chestnut.

Presently, they started to leave. Armande reminded him of tomorrow's excursion. Julia shook hands with him and begged him to pray for her when she would be saying to that very passionate, very prominent poet *je t'aime* in Russian which sounded in English (gargling with the phrase) 'yellow blue tibia'. They parted. The two girls got into Julia's smart little car. Hugh Person started walking back to his hotel, but then pulled up short with a curse and went back to retrieve his parcel.

14

Friday morning. A quick Coke. A belch. A hurried shave. He put on his ordinary clothes, throwing in the turtleneck for style. Last interview with the mirror. He plucked a black hair out of a red nostril.

The first disappointment of the day awaited him on the stroke of seven at their rendezvous (the post-office square), where he found her attended by three young athletes, Jack, Jake, and Jacques, whose copper faces he had seen grinning around her in one of the latest photographs of the fourth album. Upon noticing the sullen way his Adam's apple kept working she gaily suggested that perhaps he did not care to join them after all 'because we want to walk up to the only cable car that works in summer and that's quite a climb if you're not used to it'. White-toothed Jacques, half-embracing the pert maiden, remarked confidentially that *monsieur* should change into sturdier brogues, but Hugh retorted that in the States one hiked in any old pair of shoes, even sneakers. 'We hoped,' said Armande, 'we might induce you to learn skiing: we keep all the gear up there, with the fellow who runs the place, and he's sure to find something for you. You'll be making tempo turns in five lessons. Won't you, Percy? I think you should also need a parka, it may be summer here, at two thousand feet, but you'll find polar conditions at over nine thousand.' 'The little one is right,' said Jacques with feigned admiration, patting her on the shoulder. 'It's a forty-minute saunter,' said one of the twins. 'Limbers you up for the slopes.'

It soon transpired that Hugh would not be able to keep

53

up with them and reach the four-thousand-foot mark to catch the gondola just north of Witt. The promised 'stroll' proved to be a horrible hike, worse than anything he had experienced on school picnics in Vermont or New Hampshire. The trail consisted of very steep ups and very slippery downs, and gigantic ups again, along the side of the next mountain, and was full of old ruts, rocks, and roots. He labored, hot, wretched Hugh, behind Armande's blond bun, while she lightly followed light Jacques. The English twins made up the rear guard. Possibly, had the pace been a little more leisurely, Hugh might have managed that simple climb, but his heartless and mindless companions swung on without mercy, practically bounding up the steep bits and zestfully sliding down the declivities, which Hugh negotiated with outspread arms, in an attitude of entreaty. He refused to borrow the stick he was offered, but finally, after twenty minutes of torment, pleaded for a short breathing spell. To his dismay not Armande but Jack and Jake stayed with him as he sat on a stone, bending his head and panting, a pearl of sweat hanging from his pointed nose. They were taciturn twins and now merely exchanged silent glances as they stood a little above him on the trail, arms akimbo. He felt their sympathy ebbing and begged them to continue on their way, he would follow shortly. When they had gone he waited a little and then limped back to the village. At one spot between two forested stretches he rested again, this time on an open bluff where a bench, eyeless but eager, faced an admirable view. As he sat there smoking, he noticed his party very high above him, blue, gray, pink, red, waving to him from a cliff. He waved back and resumed his gloomy retreat.

But Hugh Person refused to give up. Mightily shod, alpenstocked, munching gum, he again accompanied them next morning. He begged them to let him set his own pace, without waiting for him anywhere, and he would have reached the cableway had he not lost his bearings and ended up in a brambly burn at the end of a logging road. Another attempt a day or two later was more successful. He almost reached timberline – but there the weather changed, a damp fog enveloped him, and he spent a couple of hours shivering all alone in a smelly shippon, waiting for the whirling mists to uncover the sun once more.

Another time he volunteered to carry after her a pair of new skis she had just acquired – weird-looking, reptile-green things made of metal and fiberglass. Their elaborate bindings looked like first cousins of orthopedic devices meant to help a cripple to walk. He was allowed to shoulder those precious skis, which at first felt miraculously light but soon grew as heavy as great slabs of malachite, under which he staggered in Armande's wake like a clown helping to change properties in a circus arena. His load was snatched from him as soon as he sat down for a rest. He was offered a paper bag (four small oranges) in exchange but he pushed it away without looking.

Our Person was obstinate and monstrously in love. A fairy-tale element seemed to imbue with its Gothic rose water all attempts to scale the battlements of her Dragon. Next week he made it and thereafter established himself as less of a nuisance.

15

As he sat sipping rum on the sun terrace of the Café du Glacier below Drakonita Hut and rather smugly contemplated, with the exhilaration of liquor in the mountain air, the skiing area (such a magic sight after so much water and matted grass!); as he took in the glaze of the upper runs, the blue herringbones lower down, the varicolored little figures outlined by the brush of chance against the brilliant white as if by a Flemish master's hand, Hugh told himself that this might make an admirable jacket design for *Christies and Other Lassies*, a great skier's autobiography (thoroughly revised and enriched by a number of hands in the office), the typescript of which he had recently copyedited, querying, as he now recalled, such terms as '*godilles*' and '*wedeln*' (rom ?). It was fun to peer over one's third drink at the painted little people skimming along, losing a ski here, a pole there, or victoriously veering in a spray of silver powder. Hugh Person, now shifting to kirsch, wondered if he could force himself to follow her advice ('such a nice big slouchy sporty-looking Yank and can't ski!') and identify himself with this or that chap charging straight down in a stylish crouch, or else be doomed to repeat for ever and ever the after-fall pause of a bulky novice asprawl on his back in hopeless, good-humored repose.

He never could pinpoint, with his dazzled and watery eyes, Armande's silhouette among the skiers. Once, however, he was sure he had caught her, floating and flashing, red-anoraked, bare-headed, agonizingly graceful, there,

there, and now there, jumping a bump, shooting down nearer and nearer, going into a tuck – and abruptly changing into a goggled stranger.

Presently she appeared from another side of the terrace, in glossy green nylon, carrying her skis, but with her formidable boots still on. He had spent enough time studying skiwear in Swiss shops to know that shoe leather had been replaced by plastic, and laces by rigid clips. 'You look like the first girl on the moon,' he said, indicating her boots, and if they had not been especially close fitting she would have wiggled her toes inside as a woman does when her footwear happens to be discussed in flattering terms (smiling toes taking over the making of mouths).

'Listen,' she said as she considered her Mondstein Sexy (their incredible trade name), 'I'll leave my skis here, and change into walking shoes and return to Witt with you *à deux*. I've quarreled with Jacques, and he has left with his dear friends. All is finished, thank God.'

Facing him in the heavenly cable car she gave a comparatively polite version of what she was to tell him a little later in disgustingly vivid detail. Jacques had demanded her presence at the onanistic sessions he held with the Blake twins at their chalet. Once already he had made Jack show her his implement but she had stamped her foot and made them behave themselves. Jacques had now presented her with an ultimatum – either she join them in their nasty games or he would cease being her lover. She was ready to be ultramodern, socially and sexually, but this was offensive, and vulgar, and as old as Greece.

The gondola would have gone on gliding forever in a blue haze sufficient for paradise had not a robust attendant stopped it before it turned to reascend for good. They got out. It was spring in the shed where the machinery performed its humble and endless duty. Armande with a prim 'excuse me' absented herself for a moment. Cows stood

57

among the dandelions outside, and radio music came from the adjacent *buvette*.

In a timid tremor of young love Hugh wondered if he might dare kiss her at some likely pause in their walk down the winding path. He would try as soon as they reached the rhododendron belt where they might stop, she to shed her parka, he to remove a pebble from his right shoe. The rhododendrons and junipers gave way to alder, and the voice of familiar despair started urging him to put off the pebble and the butterfly kiss to some later occasion. They had entered the fir forest when she stopped, looked around, and said (as casually as if she were suggesting they pick mushrooms or raspberries):

'And now one is going to make love. I know a nice mossy spot just behind those trees where we won't be disturbed, if you do it quickly.'

Orange peel marked the place. He wanted to embrace her in the preliminaries required by his nervous flesh (the 'quickly' was a mistake) but she withdrew with a fishlike flip of the body, and sat down on the whortleberries to take off her shoes and trousers. He was further dismayed by the ribbed fabric of thick-knit black tights that she wore under her ski pants. She consented to pull them down only just as far as necessary. Nor did she let him kiss her, or caress her thighs.

'Well, bad luck,' she said finally but as she twisted against him trying to draw up her tights, he regained all at once the power to do what was expected of him.

'One will go home now,' she remarked immediately afterward in her usual neutral tone, and in silence they continued their brisk downhill walk.

At the next turn of the trail the first orchard of Witt appeared at their feet, and farther down one could see the glint of a brook, a lumberyard, mown fields, brown cottages.

'I hate Witt,' said Hugh. 'I hate life. I hate myself. I hate that beastly old bench.' She stopped to look the way his fierce finger pointed, and he embraced her. At first she tried to evade his lips but he persisted desperately. All at once she gave in, and the minor miracle happened. A shiver of tenderness rippled her features, as a breeze does a reflection. Her eyelashes were wet, her shoulders shook in his clasp. That moment of soft agony was never to be repeated – or rather would never be granted the time to come back again after completing the cycle innate in its rhythm; yet that brief vibration in which she dissolved with the sun, the cherry trees, the forgiven landscape, set the tone for his new existence with its sense of 'all-is-well' despite her worst moods, her silliest caprices, her harshest demands. That kiss, and not anything preceding it, was the real beginning of their courtship.

She disengaged herself without a word. A long file of little boys followed by a scoutmaster climbed toward them along the steep path. One of them hoisted himself on an adjacent round rock and jumped down with a cheerful squeal. '*Grüss Gott*,' said their teacher in passing by Armande and Hugh. 'Hello there,' responded Hugh. 'He'll think you're crazy,' said she.

Through a beech grove and across a river, they reached the outskirts of Witt. A short cut down a muddy slope between half-built chalets took them to Villa Nastia. Anastasia Petrovna was in the kitchen, placing flowers in vases. 'Come here, Mamma,' cried Armande '*Zheniha privela*, I've brought my fiancé.'

16

Witt had a new tennis court. One day Armande challenged
Hugh to a set.

Ever since childhood and its nocturnal fears, sleep had
been our Person's habitual problem. The problem was two-
fold. He was obliged, sometimes for hours, to woo the black
automaton with an automatic repetition of some active image – that was one trouble. The other referred to the quasi-
insane state into which sleep put him, once it did come. He
could not believe that decent people had the sort of obscene
and absurd nightmares which shattered his night and continued to tingle throughout the day. Neither the incidental
accounts of bad dreams reported by friends nor the case
histories in Freudian dream books, with their hilarious
elucidations, presented anything like the complicated vile-
ness of his almost nightly experience.

In his adolescence he attempted to solve the first part of
the problem by an ingenious method which worked better
than pills (these if too mild induced too little sleep, and if
strong enhanced the vividness of monstrous visions). The
method he hit upon was repeating in mind with metro-
nomic precision the successive strokes of an outdoor game.
The only game he had ever played in his youth and could
still play at forty was tennis. Not only did he play tolerably
well, with a certain easy stylishness (caught years ago from
a dashing cousin who coached the boys at the New England
school of which his father had been headmaster), but he
had invented a shot which neither Guy, nor Guy's brother-
in-law, an even finer professional, could either make or

take. It had an element of art-for-art's sake about it, since it could not deal with low, awkward balls, required an ideally balanced stance (not easy to assume in a hurry) and, by itself, never won him a match. The Person Stroke was executed with a rigid arm and blended a vigorous drive with a clinging cut that followed the ball from the moment of impact to the end of the stroke. The impact (and this was the nicest part) had to occur at the far end of the racket's netting, with the performer standing well away from the bounce of the ball and as it were reaching out for it. The bounce had to be fairly high for the head of the racket to adhere properly, without a shadow of 'twist', and then to propel the 'glued' ball in a stiff trajectory. If the 'cling' was not enduring enough or if it started too proximally, in the middle of the racket, the result was a very ordinary, floppy, slow-curving 'galosh', quite easy, of course, to return; but when controlled accurately, the stroke reverberated with a harsh crack throughout one's forearm and whizzed off in a strongly controlled, very straight skim to a point near the baseline. On hitting the ground it clung to it in a way felt to be of the same order as the adherence of the ball to the strings during the actual stroke. While retaining its direct velocity, the ball hardly rose from the ground; in fact, Person believed that, with tremendous, all-consuming practice, the shot could be made not to bounce at all but roll with lightning speed along the surface of the court. Nobody could return an unbouncing ball, and no doubt in the near future such shots would be ruled out as illegal spoilsports. But even in its inventor's rough version it could be delightfully satisfying. The return was invariably botched in a most ludicrous fashion, because of the low-darting ball refusing to be scooped up, let alone properly hit. Guy and the other Guy were intrigued and annoyed whenever Hugh managed to bring off his 'cling drive' – which unfortunately for him was not often. He recouped himself by not telling the puzzled professionals, who tried to imitate the stroke (and achieved merely a feeble spin), that the trick lay not in the cut but in the cling, and not only in the cling itself but in the place where it occurred at the head of the strings as well as in the rigidity of the reaching-out movement of the arm. Hugh treasured his stroke mentally for years, long after the chances to use it dwindled to one or two shots in a desultory game. (In fact, the last time he executed it was that day at Witt with Armande, whereupon she walked off the court and could not be coaxed back.) Its chief use had been a means of putting himself to sleep. In those pre-dormitory exercises he greatly perfected his stroke, such as quickening its preparation (when tackling a fast serve) and learning to reproduce its mirror image backhandedly (instead of running around the ball like a fool). No sooner had he found a comfortable place for his cheek on a cool soft pillow than the familiar firm thrill would start running through his arm, and he would be slamming his way through one game after another. There were additional trimmings: explaining to a sleepy reporter, 'Cut it hard and yet keep it intact'; or winning in a mist of well-being the Davis Cup brimming with the poppy.

Why did he give up that specific remedy for insomnia when he married Armande? Surely not because she criticized his pet stroke as an insult and a bore? Was it the novelty of the shared bed, and the presence of another brain humming near his, that disturbed the privacy of the somnorific – and rather sophomoric – routine? Perhaps. Anyhow he gave up trying, persuaded himself that one or two entirely sleepless nights per week constituted for him a harmless norm, and on other nights contented himself with reviewing the events of the day (an automaton in its own right), the cares and *misères* of routine life with now and then the peacock spot that prison psychiatrists called 'having sex'.

He had said that on top of the trouble in going to sleep, he experienced dream anguish?

Dream anguish was right! He might vie with the best lunatics in regard to the recurrence of certain nightmare themes. In some cases he could establish a first rough draft, with versions following in well-spaced succession, changing in minute detail, polishing the plot, introducing some new repulsive situation, yet every time rewriting a version of the same, otherwise inexisting, story. Let's hear the repulsive part. Well, one erotic dream in particular had kept recurring with cretinous urgency over a period of several years, before and after Armande's death. In that dream which the psychiatrist (a weirdie, son of an unknown soldier and a Gypsy mother) dismissed as 'much too direct', he was offered a sleeping beauty on a great platter garnished with flowers, and a choice of tools on a cushion. These differed in length and breadth, and their number and assortment varied from dream to dream. They lay in a row, neatly aligned: a yard-long one of vulcanized rubber with a violet head, then a thick short burnished bar, then again a thin-nish skewerlike affair, with rings of raw meat and translucent lard alternating, and so on – these are random samples. There was not much sense in selecting one rather than another – the coral or the bronze, or the terrible rubber – since whatever he took changed in shape and size, and could not be properly fitted to his own anatomical system, breaking off at the burning point or snapping in two between the legs or bones of the more or less disarticulated lady. He desired to stress the following point with the fullest, fiercest, anti-Freudian force. Those oneiric torments had nothing to do, either directly or in a 'symbolic' sense, with anything he had experienced in conscious life. The erotic theme was just one theme among others, as *A Boy for Pleasure* remained just an extrinsic whimsy in relation to the whole fiction of the serious, too serious writer who had been satirized in a recent novel.

In another no less ominous nocturnal experience, he would find himself trying to stop or divert a trickle of grain or fine gravel from a rift in the texture of space and being hampered in every conceivable respect by cobwebby, splintery, filamentary elements, confused heaps and hollows, brittle debris, collapsing colossuses. He was finally blocked by masses of rubbish, and *that* was death. Less frightening but perhaps imperiling a person's brain to an even greater extent were the 'avalanche' nightmares at the rush of awakening when their imagery turned into the movement of verbal colluvia in the valleys of Toss and Thurn, whose gray rounded rocks, *Roches étonnées*, are so termed because of their puzzled and grinning surface, marked by dark 'goggles' (*écarquillages*). Dream-man is an idiot not wholly devoid of animal cunning; the fatal flaw in his mind corresponds to the splutter produced by tongue twisters: 'the risks scoundrels take'.

He was told what a pity he had not seen his analyst as soon as the nightmares grew worse. He replied he did not own one. Very patiently the doctor rejoined that the pronoun had been used not possessively but domestically as, for example, in advertisements: 'Ask your grocer'. Had Armande ever consulted an analyst? If that was a reference to Mrs Person and not to a child or a cat, then the answer was no. As a girl she seemed to have been interested in Neobuddhism and that sort of stuff, but in America new friends urged her to get, what you call, analyzed and she said she might try it after completing her Oriental studies.

He was advised that in calling her by her first name one simply meant to induce an informal atmosphere. One always did that. Only yesterday one had put another prisoner completely at ease by saying: You'd better tell Uncle your dreams or you might burn. Did Hugh, or rather Mr Person, have 'destructive urges' in his dreams – this was something that had not been made sufficiently clear. The term itself might not be sufficiently clear. A sculptor could sublimate the destructive urge by attacking an inanimate object with chisel and hammer. Major surgery offered one of the most useful means of draining off the destructive urge: a respected though not always lucky practitioner had admitted privately how difficult he found it to stop himself from hacking out every organ in sight during an operation. Everyone had secret tensions stored up from infancy. Hugh need not be ashamed of them. In fact at puberty sexual desire arises as a substitute for the desire to kill, which one normally fulfills in one's dreams; and insomnia is merely the fear of becoming aware in sleep of one's unconscious desires for slaughter and sex. About eighty percent of all dreams enjoyed by adult males are sexual. See Clarissa Dark's findings – she investigated singlehanded some two hundred healthy jailbirds whose terms of imprisonment were shortened, of course, by the number of nights spent in the Center's dormitory. Well, one hundred seventy-eight of the men were seen to have powerful erections during the stage of sleep called H A R E M ('Has A Rapid Eye Movement') marked by visions causing a lustful ophthalmic roll, a kind of internal ogling. By the way, when did Mr Person begin to hate Mrs Person? No answer. Was hate, maybe, part of his feeling for her from the very first moment? No answer. Did he ever buy her a turtleneck sweater? No answer. Was he annoyed when she found it too tight at the throat?

'I shall vomit,' said Hugh, 'if you persist in pestering me with all that odious rot.'

17

We shall now discuss love.

What powerful words, what weapons, are stored up in the mountains, at suitable spots, in special caches of the granite heart, behind painted surfaces of steel made to resemble the mottling of the adjacent rocks! But when moved to express his love, in the days of brief courtship and marriage, Hugh Person did not know where to look for words that would convince her, that would touch her, that would bring bright tears to her hard dark eyes! Per contra, something he said by chance, not planning the pang and the poetry, some trivial phrase, would prompt suddenly a hysterically happy response on the part of that dry-souled, essentially unhappy woman. Conscious attempts failed. If, as happened sometimes, at the grayest of hours, without the remotest sexual intent, he interrupted his reading to walk into her room and advance toward her on his knees and elbows like an ecstatic, undescribed, unarboreal sloth, howling his adoration, cool Armande would tell him to get up and stop playing the fool. The most ardent addresses he could think up – my princess, my sweetheart, my angel, my animal, my exquisite beast – merely exasperated her. 'Why,' she inquired, 'can't you talk to me in a natural human manner, as a gentleman talks to a lady, why must you put on such a clownish act, why can't you be serious, and plain, and believable?' But love, he said, was anything but believable, real life *was* ridiculous, yokels laughed at love. He tried to kiss the hem of her skirt or bite the crease of her trouserleg, her instep, the toe of her furious foot –

and as he groveled, his unmusical voice muttering maudlin, exotic, rare, common nothings and everythings, into his own ear, as it were, the simple expression of love became a kind of degenerate avian performance executed by the male alone, with no female in sight – long neck straight, then curved, beak dipped, neck straightened again. It all made him ashamed of himself but he could not stop and she could not understand, for at such times he never came up with the right word, the right waterweed.

He loved her in spite of her unlovableness. Armande had many trying, though not necessarily rare, traits, all of which he accepted as absurd clues in a clever puzzle. She called her mother, to her face, *skotina*, 'brute' – not being aware, naturally, that she would never see her again after leaving with Hugh for New York and death. She liked to give carefully planned parties, and no matter how long ago this or that gracious gathering had taken place (ten months, fifteen months, or even earlier before her marriage, at her mother's house in Brussels or Witt) every party and topic remained for ever preserved in the humming frost of her tidy mind. She visualized those parties in retrospect as stars on the veil of the undulating past, and saw her guests as the extremities of her own personality: vulnerable points that had to be treated thenceforth with nostalgic respect. If Julia or June remarked casually that they had never met art critic C. (the late Charles Chamar's cousin), whereas both Julia and June had attended the party, as registered in Armande's mind, she might get very nasty, denouncing the mistake in a disdainful drawl, and adding, with belly-dance contortions: 'In that case you must have forgotten also the little sandwiches from Père Igor' (some special shop) 'which you enjoyed so much.' Hugh had never seen such a vile temper, such morbid *amour-propre*, so self-centered a nature. Julia, who had skied and skated with her, thought her a darling, but most women criticized her, and in telephone chats with one another mimicked her rather pathetic little tricks of attack and retort. If anybody started to say 'Shortly before I broke my leg –' she would chime in with the triumphant: 'And I broke both in my childhood!' For some occult reason she used an ironic and on the whole disagreeable tone of voice when addressing her husband in public.

She had strange whims. During their honeymoon in Stresa, on their last night there (his New York office was clamoring for his return), she decided that last nights were statistically the most dangerous ones in hotels without fire escapes, and their hotel looked indeed most combustible, in a massive old-fashioned way. For some reason or other, television producers consider that there is nothing more photogenic and universally fascinating than a good fire. Armande, viewing the Italian telenews, had been upset or feigned to be upset (she was fond of making herself interesting) by one such calamity on the local screen – little flames like slalom flaglets, huge ones like sudden demons, water squirting in intersecting curves like so many rococo fountains, and fearless men in glistening oilskin who directed all sorts of muddled operations in a fantasy of smoke and destruction. That night at Stresa she insisted they rehearse (he in his sleeping shorts, she in a Chudo-Yudo pajama) an acrobatic escape in the stormy murk by climbing down the overdecorated face of their hotel, from the fourth story to the second one, and thence to the roof of a gallery amidst tossing remonstrative trees. Hugh vainly reasoned with her. The spirited girl affirmed that as an expert rock-climber she knew it could be done by using footholds which various applied ornaments, generous juttings, and little railed balconies here and there provided for one's careful descent. She ordered Hugh to follow her and train an electric torch on her from above. He was also supposed to keep close enough to help her if need be by holding her suspended, and thus increased in vertical length, while she probed the next step with a bare toe.

Hugh, despite forelimb strength, was a singularly inept anthropoid. He badly messed up the exploit. He got stuck on a ledge just under their balcony. His flashlight played erratically over a small part of the façade before slipping from his grasp. He called down from his perch entreating her to return. Underfoot a shutter opened abruptly. Hugh managed to scramble back onto his balcony, still roaring her name, though persuaded by now that she had perished. Eventually, however, she was located in a third-floor room where he found her wrapped up in a blanket smoking peacefully, supine on the bed of a stranger, who sat in a chair by the bed, reading a magazine.

Her sexual oddities perplexed and distressed Hugh. He put up with them during their trip. They became routine stuff when he returned with a difficult bride to his New York apartment. Armande decreed they regularly make love around teatime, in the living room, as upon an imaginary stage, to the steady accompaniment of casual small talk, with both performers decently clothed, he wearing his best business suit and a polka-dotted tie, she a smart black dress closed at the throat. In concession to nature, undergarments could be parted, or even undone, but only very, very discreetly, without the least break in the elegant chit-chat: impatience was pronounced unseemly, exposure, monstrous. A newspaper or coffee-table book hid such preparations as he absolutely had to conduct, wretched Hugh, and woe to him if he winced or fumbled during the actual commerce; but far worse than the awful pull of long underwear in the chaos of his pinched crotch or the crisp contact with her armor-smooth stockings was the prerequisite of light colloquy, about acquaintances, or politics, or zodiacal signs, or servants, and in the meantime, with visible hurry banned, the poignant work had to be brought surreptitiously to a convulsive end in a twisted half-sitting position on an uncomfortable little divan. Hugh's mediocre potency might not have survived the ordeal had she concealed from him more completely than she thought she did the excitement derived from the contrast between the fictitious and the factual – a contrast which after all has certain claims to artistic subtlety if we recall the customs of certain Far Eastern people, virtually halfwits in many other respects. But his chief support lay in the never deceived expectancy of the dazed ecstasy that gradually idiotized her dear features, notwithstanding her efforts to maintain the flippant patter. In a sense he preferred the parlor setting to the even less normal decor of those rare occasions when she desired him to possess her in bed, well under the bedclothes, while she telephoned, gossiping with a female friend or hoaxing an unknown male. Our Person's capacity to condone all this, to find reasonable explanations and so forth, endears him to us, but also provokes limpid mirth, alas, at times. For example, he told himself that she refused to strip because she was shy of her tiny pouting breasts and the scar of a ski accident along her thigh. Silly Person!

Was she faithful to him throughout the months of their marriage spent in frail, lax, merry America? During their first and last winter there she went a few times to ski without him, at Aval, Quebec, or Chute, Colorado. While alone, he forbade himself to dwell in thought on the banalities of betrayal, such as holding hands with a chap or permitting him to kiss her good night. Those banalities were to him quite as excruciating to imagine as would be voluptuous intercourse. A steel door of the spirit remained securely shut as long as she was away, but no sooner had she arrived, her face brown and shiny, her figure as trim as that of an air hostess, in that blue coat with flat buttons as bright as counters of gold, than something ghastly opened up in him and a dozen lithe athletes started swarming around and prying her apart in all the motels of his mind, although actually, as we know, she had enjoyed full conjunction with only a dozen crack lovers in the course of three trips.

Nobody, least of all her mother, could understand why Armande married a rather ordinary American with a not very solid job, but we must end now our discussion of love.

18

In the second week of February, about one month before death separated them, the Persons flew over to Europe for a few days: Armande, to visit her mother dying in a Belgian hospital (the dutiful daughter came too late), and Hugh, at his firm's request, to look up Mr R. and another American writer, also residing in Switzerland.

It was raining hard when a taxi deposited him in front of R.'s big, old, and ugly country house above Versex. He made his way up a graveled path between streams of bubbly rainwater running on both sides of it. He found the front door ajar, and while tramping the mat noticed with amused surprise Julia Moore standing with her back to him at the telephone table in the vestibule. She now wore again the pretty pageboy hairdo of the past and the same orange blouse. He had finished wiping his feet when she put back the receiver and turned out to be a totally different girl.

'Sorry to have made you wait,' she said, fixing on him a pair of smiling eyes. 'I'm replacing Mr Tamworth, who is vacationing in Morocco.'

Hugh Person entered the library, a comfortably furnished but decidedly old-fashioned and quite inadequately lighted room, lined with encyclopedias, dictionaries, directories, and the author's copies of the author's books in multiple editions and translations. He sat down in a club chair and drew a list of points to be discussed from his briefcase. The two main questions were: how to alter certain much too recognizable people in the typescript of *Tralatitions* and what to do with that commercially impossible title.

Presently R. came in. He had not shaved for three or four days and wore ridiculous blue overalls which he found convenient for distributing about him the tools of his profession, such as pencils, ball pens, three pairs of glasses, cards, jumbo clips, elastic bands, and – in an invisible state – the dagger which after a few words of welcome he pointed at our Person.

'I can only repeat,' he said, collapsing in the armchair vacated by Hugh and motioning him to a similar one opposite, 'what I said not once but often already: you can alter a cat but you cannot alter my characters. As to the title, which is a perfectly respectable synonym of the word "metaphor", no savage steeds will pull it from under me. My doctor advised Tamworth to lock up my cellar, which he did and concealed the key which the locksmith will not be able to duplicate before Monday and I'm too proud, you know, to buy the cheap wines they have in the village, so all I can offer you – you shake your head in advance and you're jolly right, son – is a can of apricot juice. Now allow me to talk to you about titles and libels. You know, that letter you wrote me tickled me black in the face. I have been accused of trifling with minors, but my minor characters are untouchable, if you permit me a pun.'

He went on to explain that if your true artist had chosen to form a character on the basis of a living individual, any rewriting aimed at disguising that character was tantamount to destroying the living prototype as would driving, you know, a pin through a little doll of clay, and the girl next door falls dead. If the composition was artistic, if it held not only water but wine, then it was invulnerable in one sense and horribly fragile in another. Fragile, because when a timid editor made the artist change 'slender' to 'plump', or 'brown' to 'blond' he disfigured both the image and the niche where it stood and the entire chapel around it; and invulnerable, because no matter how drastically

73

you changed the image, its prototype would remain recognizable by the shape of the hole left in the texture of the tale. But apart from all that, the customers whom he was accused of portraying were much too cool to announce their presence and their resentment. In fact they would rather enjoy listening to the tattle in literary salons with a little knowing air, as the French say.

The question of the title – *Tralatitions* – was another kettle of fish. Readers did not realize that two types of title existed. One type was the title found by the dumb author or the clever publisher after the book had been written. *That* was simply a label stuck on and tapped with the side of the fist. Most of our worst best-sellers had that kind of title. But there was the other kind: the title that shone through the book like a watermark, the title that was born with the book, the title to which the author had grown so accustomed during the years of accumulating the written pages that it had become part of each and of all. No, Mr R. could not give up *Tralatitions*.

Hugh made bold to remark that the tongue tended to substitute an 'l' for the second of the three 't's'.

'The tongue of ignorance,' shouted Mr R.

His pretty little secretary tripped in and announced that he should not get excited or tired. The great man rose with an effort and stood quivering and grinning, and proffering a large hairy hand.

'Well,' said Hugh, 'I shall certainly tell Phil how strongly you feel about the points he has raised. Good-bye, sir, you will be getting a sample of the jacket design next week.'

'So long and soon see,' said Mr R.

19

We are back in New York and this is their last evening together.

After serving them an excellent supper (a little on the rich side, perhaps, but not overabundant – neither was a big eater) obese Pauline, the *femme de ménage*, whom they shared with a Belgian artist in the penthouse immediately above them, washed the dishes and left at her usual hour (nine fifteen or thereabouts). Since she had the annoying propensity of sitting down for a moment to enjoy a bit of T.V, Armande always waited for her to have gone before running it for her own pleasure. She now turned it on, let it live for a moment, changed channels – and killed the picture with a snort of disgust (her likes and dislikes in these matters lacked all logic, she might watch one or two programs with passionate regularity or on the contrary not touch the set for a week as if punishing that marvelous invention for a misdemeanor known only to her, and Hugh preferred to ignore her obscure feuds with actors and commentators). She opened a book, but here Phil's wife rang up to invite her on the morrow to the preview of a Lesbian drama with a Lesbian cast. Their conversation lasted twenty-five minutes, Armande using a confidential undertone, and Phyllis speaking so sonorously that Hugh, who sat at a round table correcting a batch of galleys, could have heard, had he felt so inclined, both sides of the trivial torrent. He contented himself instead with the résumé Armande gave him upon returning to the settee of gray plush near the fake fireplace. As had happened on previous occasions, around ten o'clock a most jarring succession of bumps and scrapes suddenly came from above: it was the cretin upstairs dragging a heavy piece of inscrutable sculpture (catalogued as *Pauline anide*') from the center of his studio to the corner it occupied at night. In invariable response, Armande glared at the ceiling and remarked that in the case of a less amiable and helpful neighbor she would have complained long ago to Phil's cousin (who managed the apartment house). When placidity was restored, she started to look for the book she had had in her hand before the telephone rang. Her husband always felt a flow of special tenderness that reconciled him to the boring or brutal ugliness of what not very happy people call 'life' every time that he noted in neat, efficient, clear-headed Armande the beauty and helplessness of human abstraction. He now found the object of her pathetic search (it was in the magazine rack near the telephone) and, as he restored it to her, he was allowed to touch with reverent lips her temple and a strand of blond hair. Then he went back to the galleys of *Tralatitions* and she to her book, which was a French touring guide that listed many splendid restaurants, forked and starred, but not many 'pleasant, quiet, well-situated hotels' with three or more turrets and sometimes a little red songbird on a twig.

'Here's a cute coincidence,' observed Hugh. 'One of his characters, in a rather bawdy passage – by the way should it be "Savoie" or "Savoy"?'

'What's the coincidence?'

'Oh. One of his characters is consulting a Michelin, and says: there's many a mile between Condom in Gascogne and Pussy in Savoie.'

'The Savoy is a hotel,' said Armande and yawned twice, first with clenched jaws, then openly. 'I don't know why I'm so tired,' she added, 'but I know all this yawning only sidetracks sleep. I think I'll sample my new tablets tonight.'

'Try imagining you're skimming on skis down a very smooth slope. I used to play tennis mentally when I was young and it often helped, especially with new, very white balls.'

She remained seated, lost in thought, for another moment, then red-ribboned the place and went for a glass to the kitchen.

Hugh liked to read a set of proofs twice, once for the defects of the type and once for the virtues of the text. It worked better, he believed, if the eye check came first and the mind's pleasure next. He was now enjoying the latter and while not looking for errors, still had a chance to catch a missed boo-boo – his own or the printer's. He also permitted himself to query, with the utmost diffidence, in the margin of a second copy (meant for the author), certain idiosyncrasies of style and spelling, hoping the great man would understand that not genius but grammar was being questioned.

After a long consultation with Phil it had been decided not to do anything about the risks of defamation involved in the frankness with which R. described his complicated love life. He had 'paid for it once in solitude and remorse, and now was ready to pay in hard cash any fool whom his story might hurt' (abridged and simplified citation from his latest letter). In a long chapter of a much more libertine nature (despite the grandiose wording) than the jock talk of the fashionable writers he criticized, R. showed a mother and daughter regaling their young lover with spectacular caresses on a mountain ledge above a scenic chasm and in other less perilous spots. Hugh did not know Mrs R. intimately enough to assess her resemblance to the matron of the book (loppy breasts, flabby thighs, coon-bear grunts during copulation, and so forth); but the daughter in manner and movement, in breathless speech, in many other features with which he was not consciously familiar but which fitted the picture, was certainly Julia, although the author *had* made her fair-haired, and played down the Eurasian quality of her beauty. Hugh read with interest and concentration, but through the translucidity of the textual flow he still was correcting proof as some of us try to do – mending a broken letter here, indicating italics there, his eye and his spine (the true reader's main organ) collaborating rather than occluding each other. Sometimes he wondered what the phrase really meant – what exactly did 'rimiform' suggest and how did a 'balanic plum' look, or should he cap the 'b' and insert a 'k' after 'l'? The dictionary he used at home was less informative than the huge battered one in the office and he was now stumped by such beautiful things as 'all the gold of a kew tree' and 'a dappled nebris'. He queried the middle word in the name of an incidental character 'Adam von Librikov' because the German particle seemed to clash with the rest; or was the entire combination a sly scramble? He finally crossed out his query, but on the other hand reinstated the 'Reign of Cnut' in another passage: a humbler proofreader before him had supposed that either the letters in the last word should be transposed or that it be corrected to 'the Knout' – she was of Russian descent, like Armande.

Our Person, our reader, was not sure he entirely approved of R.'s luxuriant and bastard style; yet, at its best ('the gray rainbow of a fog-dogged moon'), it was diabolically evocative. He also caught himself trying to establish on the strength of fictional data at what age, in what circumstances, the writer had begun to debauch Julia: had it been in her childhood – tickling her in her bath, kissing her wet shoulders, then one day carrying her wrapped in a big towel to his lair, as delectably described in the novel? Or did he flirt with her in her first college year, when he was paid two thousand dollars for reading to an enormous gown-and-town audience some short story of his, published and republished many times before but really wonderful stuff? How good to have *that* type of talent!

20

It was past eleven by now. He put out the lights in the living room and opened the window. The windy March night found something to finger in the room. An electric sign, DOPPLER, shifted to violet through the half-drawn curtains and illumined the deadly white papers he had left on the table.

He let his eyes get used to the obscurity in the next room, and presently stole in. Her first sleep was marked usually by a clattering snore. One could not help marveling how such a slender and dainty girl could churn up so ponderous a vibration. It had bothered Hugh at the early stage of their marriage because of the implicit threat of its going on all night. But something, some outside noise, or a jolt in her dream, or the discreet clearing of a meek husband's throat, caused her to stir, to sigh, to smack her lips, perhaps, or turn on her side, after which she slept mutely. This change of rhythm had apparently taken place while he was still working in the parlor; and now, lest the entire cycle recur, he tried to undress as quietly as possible. He later remembered pulling out very gingerly an exceptionally creaky drawer (whose voice he never noticed at other times) to get a fresh pair of the briefs which he wore in lieu of pajamas. He swore under his breath at the old wood's stupid plaint and refrained from pushing the drawer back; but the floor boards took over as soon as he started to tiptoe to his side of the double bed. Did that wake her? Yes, it did, hazily, or at least teased a hole in the hay, and she murmured something about the light. Actually all that impinged on the darkness was an angled beam from the living room, the door of which he had left ajar. He now closed it gently as he groped his way to the bed.

He lay open-eyed for a while listening to another tenacious small sound, the pinking of waterdrops on the linoleum under a defective radiator. You said you thought you were in for a sleepless night? Not exactly. He felt in fact quite sleepy, and in no need of the alarmingly effective 'Murphy Pill' which he resorted to now and then; but despite the drowsiness he was aware that a number of worries had crept up ready to pounce. What worries? Ordinary ones, nothing very serious or special. He lay on his back waiting for them to collect, which they did in unison with the pale blotches stealing up to take their accustomed position upon the ceiling as his eyes got used to the dark. He reflected that his wife was again feigning a feminine ailment to keep him away; that she probably cheated in many other ways; that he too betrayed her in a sense by concealing from her the one night spent with another girl, premaritally, in terms of time, but spatially in this very room; that preparing other people's books for publication was a debasing job; that no manner of permanent drudgery or temporary dissatisfaction mattered in the face of his ever growing, ever more tender, love for his wife; that he would have to consult an ophthalmologist sometime next mouth. He substituted an 'n' for the wrong letter and continued to scan the motley proof into which the blackness of closed vision was now turning. A double systole catapulted him into full consciousness again, and he promised his uncorrected self that he would limit his daily ration of cigarettes to a couple of heartbeats.

'And then you dropped off?'

'Yes. I may have still struggled to make out a vague line of print but – yes, I slept.'

'Fitfully, I imagine?'

'No, on the contrary, my sleep was never deeper. You see, I had not slept for more than a few minutes the night before.'

'O.K. Now I wonder if you are aware that psychologists attached to great prisons must have studied, among other things, that part of thanatology which deals with means and methods of violent death?'

Person emitted a weary negative sound.

'Well, let me put it this way: the police like to know what tool was used by the offender; the thanatologist wishes to know why and how it was used. Clear so far?'

Weary affirmative.

'Tools are, well – tools. They may, in fact, be an integral part of the worker, as, say, the carpenter's square is indeed part of the carpenter. Or the tools may be of flesh and bone like these' (taking Hugh's hands, patting each in turn, placing them on his palms for display or as if to begin some children's game).

His huge hands were returned to Hugh like two empty dishes. Next, it was explained to him that in strangling a young adult one of two methods was commonly used: the amateurish, none too efficient, frontal attack, and the more professional approach made from behind. In the first method, the eight fingers stiffly encircle the victim's neck while the two thumbs compress his or her throat; one runs, however, the risk of her or his hands seizing one's wrists or otherwise fighting off the assault. The second, much safer way, from behind, consists in pressing both thumbs hard against the back of the boy's or, preferably, girl's neck and working upon the throat with one's fingers. The first hold is dubbed among us 'Pouce', the second 'Fingerman'. We know you attacked from the rear, but the following question arises: when you planned to throttle your wife why did you choose the Fingerman? Because you instinctively. felt that its sudden and vigorous grip presented the best chance of success? Or did you have other, subjective, considerations in mind, such as thinking you'd really hate to watch her changes of facial expression during the process?

He did not plan anything. He had slept throughout the horrible automatic act, waking up only when both had landed on the floor by the bed.

He had mentioned dreaming the house was on fire?

That's right. Flames spurted all around and whatever one saw came through scarlet strips of vitreous plastic. His chance bedmate had flung the window wide open. Oh, who was she? She came from the past – a streetwalker he had picked up on his first trip abroad, some twenty years ago, a poor girl of mixed parentage, though actually American and very sweet, called Giulia Romeo, the surname means 'pilgrim' in archaic Italian, but then we all are pilgrims, and all dreams are anagrams of diurnal reality. He dashed after her to stop her from jumping out. The window was large and low; it had a broad sill padded and sheeted, as was customary in that country of ice and fire. Such glaciers, such dawns! Giulia, or Julie, wore a Doppler shift over her luminous body and prostrated herself on the sill, with outspread arms still touching the wings of the window. He glanced down across her, and there, far below, in the chasm of the yard or garden, the selfsame flames moved like those tongues of red paper which a concealed ventilator causes to flicker around imitation yule logs in the festive shop-windows of snowbound childhoods. To leap, or try to lower oneself on knotted ledgelinen (the knotting was being demonstrated by a medievalish, sort of Flemish, long-necked shopgirl in a speculum at the back of his dream), seemed to him madness, and poor Hugh did all he could to restrain Juliet. Trying for the best hold, he had clutched her around the neck from behind, his square-nailed thumbs digging into her violet-lit nape, his eight fingers compressing her throat. A writhing windpipe was being shown on a screen

83

of science cinema across the yard or street, but for the rest everything had become quite secure and comfortable: he had clamped Julia nicely and would have saved her from certain death if in her suicidal struggle to escape from the fire she had not slipped somehow over the sill and taken him with her into the void. What a fall! What a silly Julia! What luck that Mr Romeo still gripped and twisted and cracked that crooked cricoid as X-rayed by the firemen and mountain guides in the street. How they flew! Superman carrying a young soul in his embrace!

The impact of the ground was far less brutal than he had expected. This is a bravura piece and not a patient's dream, Person. I shall have to report you. He hurt his elbow, and her night table collapsed with the lamp, a tumbler, a book; but Art be praised – she was safe, she was with him, she was lying quite still. He groped for the fallen lamp and neatly lit it in its unusual position. For a moment he wondered what his wife was doing there, prone on the floor, her fair hair spread as if she were flying. Then he stared at his bashful claws.

21

Dear Phil,

This, no doubt, is my last letter to you. I am leaving you. I am leaving you for another even greater Publisher. In that House I shall be proofread by cherubim – or misprinted by devils, depending on the department my poor soul is assigned to. So adieu, dear friend, and may your heir auction this off most profitably.

Its holographical nature is explained by the fact that I prefer it not to be read by Tom Tam or one of his boy typists. I am mortally sick after a botched operation in the only private room of a Bolognese hospital. The kind young nurse who will mail it has told me with dreadful carving gestures something I paid her for as generously as I would her favors if I still were a man. Actually favors of death knowledge are infinitely more precious than those of love. According to my almond-eyed little spy, the great surgeon, may his own liver rot, lied to me when he declared yesterday with a deathhead's grin that the *operazione* had been *perfetta*. Well, it had been so in the sense Euler called zero the perfect number. Actually, they ripped me open, cast one horrified look at my decayed *fegato*, and without touching it sewed me up again.

I shall not bother you with the Tamworth problem. You should have seen the smug expression of the oblong fellow's bearded lips when he visited me this morning. As you know – as everybody, even Marion, knows – he gnawed his way into all my affairs, crawling into every cranny, collecting every German-accented word of mine, so that now he can boswell the dead man just as he had bossed very well the living one. I am also writing my and your lawyer about the measures I would like to be taken after my departure in order to thwart Tamworth at every turn of his labyrinthian plans.

The only child I have ever loved is the ravishing, silly, treacherous little Julia Moore. Every cent and centime I possess as well as all literary remains that can be twisted out of Tamworth's clutches must go to her, whatever the ambiguous obscurities contained in my will: Sam knows what I am hinting at and will act accordingly.

The last two parts of my Opus are in your hands. I am very sorry that Hugh Person is not there to look after its publication. When you acknowledge this letter do not say a word of having received it, but instead, in a kind of code that would tell me you bear in mind this letter, give me, as a good old gossip, some information about him – why, for example, was he jailed, for a year – or more? – if he was found to have acted in a purely epileptic trance; why was he transferred to an asylum for the criminal insane after his case was reviewed and no crime found? And why was he shuttled between prison and madhouse for the next five or six years before ending up as a privately treated patient? How can one treat dreams, unless one is a quack? Please tell me all this because Person was one of the nicest persons I knew and also because you can smuggle all kinds of secret information for this poor soul in your letter about him.

Poor soul is right, you know. My wretched liver is as heavy as a rejected manuscript; they manage to keep the hideous hyena pain at bay by means of frequent injections but somehow or other it remains always present *behind* the wall of my flesh like the muffled thunder of a permanent avalanche which obliterates there, beyond me, all the structures of my imagination, all the landmarks of my conscious self. It is comic – but I used to believe that dying persons saw the vanity of things, the futility of fame, passion, art, and so forth. I believed that treasured memories in a dying man's mind dwindled to rainbow wisps; but now I feel just the contrary: my most trivial sentiments and those of all men have acquired gigantic proportions. The entire solar system is but a reflection in the crystal of my (or your) wrist watch. The more I shrivel the bigger I grow. I suppose this is an uncommon phenomenon. Total rejection of all religions ever dreamt up by man and total composure in the face of total death! If I could explain this triple totality in one big book, that book would become no doubt a new bible and its author the founder of a new creed. Fortunately for my self-esteem that book will not be written – not merely because a dying man cannot write books but because that particular one would never express in one flash what can only be understood *immediately*.

Note added by the recipient:

Received on the day of the writer's death. File under Repos – R.

22

Person hated the sight and the feel of his feet. They were uncommonly graceless and sensitive. Even as a grown man he avoided looking at them when undressing. Hence he escaped the American mania of going barefoot at home – that throwback across childhood to plainer and thriftier times. What a jaggy chill he experienced at the mere thought of catching a toenail in the silk of a sock (silk socks were out, too)! Thus a woman shivers at the squeak of a rubbed pane. They were knobby, they were weak, they always hurt. Buying shoes equaled seeing the dentist. He now cast a long look of dislike at the article he had bought at Brig on the way to Witt. Nothing is ever wrapped up with such diabolical neatness as a shoebox. Ripping the paper off afforded him nervous relief. This pair of revoltingly heavy brown mountain boots had already once been tried on in the shop. They were certainly the right size, and quite as certainly they were not as comfortable as the salesman assured him they were. Snug, yes, but oppressively so. He pulled them on with a groan and laced them with imprecations. No matter, it must be endured. The climb he contemplated could not be accomplished in town shoes: the first and only time he had attempted to do so, he had kept losing his footing on slippery slabs of rock. These at least gripped treacherous surfaces. He also remembered the blisters inflicted by a similar pair, but made of chamois, that he had acquired eight years ago and thrown away when leaving Witt. Well, the left pinched a little less than the right – lame consolation.

He discarded his dark heavy jacket and put on an old windbreaker. As he went down the passage he encountered three steps before reaching the lift. The only purpose he could assign to them was that they warned him he was going to suffer. But he dismissed the little ragged edge of pain, and lit a cigarette.

Typically, in the case of a second-rate hotel, its best view of the mountains was from the corridor windows at its north end. Dark, almost black rocky heights streaked with white, some of the ridges blending with the sullen overcast sky; lower down the fur of coniferous forests, still lower the lighter green of fields. Melancholy mountains! Glorified lumps of gravity!

The floor of the valley, with the townlet of Witt and various hamlets along a narrow river, consisted of dismal small meadows, with barbed-wire fences enclosing them and with a rank flowering of tall fennel for sole ornament. The river was as straight as a canal and all smothered in alder. The eye roamed wide but found no comfort in taking in the near and the far, this muddy cowtrack athwart a mowed slope or that plantation of regimented larches on the opposite rise.

The first stage of his revisitation (Person was prone to pilgrimages as had been a French ancestor of his, a Catholic poet and well-nigh a saint) consisted of a walk through Witt to a cluster of chalets on a slope above it. The townlet itself seemed even uglier and stragglier. He recognized the fountain, and the bank, and the church, and the great chestnut tree, and the café. And there was the post office, with the bench near its door waiting for letters that never came.

He crossed the bridge without stopping to listen to the vulgar noise of the stream which could tell him nothing. The slope had a fringe of firs at the top and beyond them stood additional firs – misty phantoms or replacement trees – in a grayish array under rain clouds. A new road had been built and new houses had grown, crowding out the meager landmarks he remembered or thought he remembered.

He now had to find Villa Nastia, which still retained a dead old woman's absurd Russian diminutive. She had sold it just before her last illness to a childless English couple. He would glance at the porch, as one uses a glazed envelope to slip in an image of the past.

Hugh hesitated at a street corner. Just beyond it a woman was selling vegetables from a stall. *Est-ce que vous savez, Madame* – Yes, she did, it was up that lane. As she spoke, a large, white, shivering dog crawled from behind a crate and with a shock of futile recognition Hugh remembered that eight years ago he had stopped right here and had noticed that dog, which was pretty old even then and had now braved fabulous age only to serve his blind memory.

The surroundings were unrecognizable – except for the white wall. His heart was beating as after an arduous climb. A blond little girl with a badminton racket crouched and picked up her shuttlecock from the sidewalk. Farther up he located Villa Nastia, now painted a celestial blue. All its windows were shuttered.

23

Choosing one of the marked trails leading into the mountains, Hugh recognized another detail of the past, namely the venerable inspector of benches – bird-defiled benches as old as he – that were rotting in shady nooks here and there, brown leaves below, green leaves above, by the side of a resolutely idyllic footpath ascending toward a waterfall. He remembered the inspector's pipe studded with Bohemian gems (in harmony with its owner's furuncular nose) and also the habit Armande had of exchanging ribald comments in Swiss-German with the old fellow while he was examining the rubbish under a cracked seat.

The region now offered tourists an additional number of climbs and cableways as well as a new motorcar road from Witt to the gondola station which Armande and her friends used to reach on foot. In his day Hugh had carefully studied the public map, a great Carte du Tendre or Chart of Torture, spread out on a billboard near the post office. Had he wished now to travel in comfort to the glacier slopes he could have taken the new bus which connected Witt with the Drakonita cable car. He wanted, however, to do it the old hard way and to pass through the unforgettable forest on his way up. He hoped the Drakonita gondola would be the remembered one – a small cabin with two benches facing each other. It rode up keeping some twenty yards above a strip of turfy slope in a cutting between fir trees and alder bushes. Every thirty seconds or so it negotiated a pylon with a sudden rattle and shake but otherwise glided with dignity.

Hugh's memory had bunched into one path the several wood trails and logging roads that led to the first difficult stage of the ascent – namely, a jumble of boulders and a jungle of rhododendrons, through which one struck upward to reach the cable car. No wonder he soon lost his way.

His memory, in the meantime, kept following its private path. Again he was panting in her merciless wake. Again she was teasing Jacques, the handsome Swiss boy with fox-red body hair and dreamy eyes. Again she flirted with the eclectic English twins, who called gullies Cool Wars and ridges Ah Rates. Hugh, despite his tremendous physique, had neither the legs nor the lungs to keep up with them even in memory. And when the foursome had accelerated their climbing pace and vanished with their cruel ice axes and coils of rope and other instruments of torture (equipment exaggerated by ignorance), he rested on a rock, and, looking down, seemed to see through the moving mists the making of the very mountains that his tormentors trod, the crystalline crust heaving up with his heart from the bottom of an immemorial *more* (sea). Generally, however, he would be urged not to straggle after them even before they were out of the forest, a dismal group of old firs, with steep muddy paths and thickets of wet willow herb.

He now ascended through that wood, panting as painfully as he had in the past when following Armande's golden nape or a huge knapsack on a naked male back. As then the pressure of the shoecap upon his right foot had soon scraped off a round of skin at the joint of the third toe, resulting in a red eye burning there through every threadbare thought. He finally shook the forest off and reached a rock-strewn field and a barn that he thought he recalled, but the stream where he had once washed his feet and the broken bridge which suddenly spanned the gap of time in his mind were nowhere to be seen. He walked on. The day seemed a little brighter but presently a cloud palmed the sun again. The path had reached the pastures. He noticed a large white butterfly drop outspread on a stone. Its papery wings, blotched with black and maculated with faded crimson, had transparent margins of an unpleasant crimped texture, which shivered slightly in the cheerless wind. Hugh disliked insects; this one looked particularly gross. Nevertheless, a mood of unusual kindliness made him surmount the impulse to crush it under a blind boot. With the vague idea that it must be tired and hungry and would appreciate being transferred to a near-by pincushion of little pink flowers, he stooped over the creature but with a great shuffle and rustle it evaded his handkerchief, sloppily flapped to overcome gravity, and vigorously sailed away.

He walked up to a signpost. Forty-five minutes to Lammerspitz, two hours and a half to Rimperstein. This was not the way to the glacier gondola. The distances indicated seemed as dull as delirium.

Round-browed gray rocks with patches of black moss and pale-green lichen lined the trail beyond the signpost. He looked at the clouds blurring the distant peaks or sagging like blubber between them. It was not worthwhile continuing that lone climb. Had she passed here, had her soles once imprinted their elaborate pattern in that clay? He considered the remnants of a solitary picnic, bits of eggshell broken off by the fingers of another solitary hiker who had sat here a few minutes ago, and a crumpled plastic bag into which a succession of rapid feminine hands had once conveyed with tiny tongs white apple roundlets, black prunes, nuts, raisins, the sticky mummy of a banana – all this digested by now. The grayness of rain would soon engulf everything. He felt a first kiss on his bald spot and walked back to the woods and widowhood.

Days like this give sight a rest and allow other senses to function more freely. Earth and sky were drained of all color. It was either raining or pretending to rain or not raining at all, yet still appearing to rain in a sense that only certain old Northern dialects can either express verbally or not express, but *versionize*, as it were, through the ghost of a sound produced by a drizzle in a haze of grateful rose shrubs. 'Raining in Wittenberg, but not in Wittgenstein.' An obscure joke in *Tralatitions*.

24

Direct interference in a person's life does not enter our scope of activity, nor, on the other, tralatitiously speaking, hand, is his destiny a chain of predeterminate links: some 'future' events may be likelier than others, O.K., but all are chimeric, and every cause-and-effect sequence is always a hit-and-miss affair, even if the lunette has actually closed around your neck, and the cretinous crowd holds its breath.

Only chaos would result if some of us championed Mr X, while another group backed Miss Julia Moore, whose interests, such as distant dictatorships, turned out to clash with those of her ailing old suitor Mr (now Lord) X. The most we can do when steering a favorite in the best direction, in circumstances not involving injury to others, is to act as a breath of wind and to apply the lightest, the most indirect pressure such as *trying* to induce a dream that we *hope* our favorite will recall as prophetic if a likely event does actually happen. On the printed page the words 'likely' and 'actually' should be italicized too, at least *slightly*, to indicate a *slight* breath of wind inclining those characters (in the sense of both signs and personae). In fact, we depend on italics to an even greater degree than do, in their arch quaintness, writers of children's books.

Human life can be compared to a person dancing in a variety of forms around his own self: thus the vegetables of our first picture book encircled a boy in his dream – green cucumber, blue eggplant, red beet, Potato *père*, Potato *fils*, a girly asparagus, and, oh, many more, their spinning *ronde* going faster and faster and gradually forming a transparent ring of banded colors around a dead person or planet.

Another thing we are not supposed to do is to explain the inexplicable. Men have learned to live with a black burden, a huge aching hump: the supposition that 'reality' may be only a 'dream'. How much more dreadful it would be if the very awareness of your being aware of reality's dreamlike nature were also a dream, a built-in hallucination! One should bear in mind, however, that there is no mirage without a vanishing point, just as there is no lake without a closed circle of reliable land.

We have shown our need for quotation marks ('reality', 'dream'). Decidedly, the signs with which Hugh Person still peppers the margins of galleys have a metaphysical or zodiacal import! 'Dust to dust' (the dead are good mixers, that's quite certain, at least). A patient in one of Hugh's mental hospitals, a bad man but a good philosopher, who was at that time terminally ill (hideous phrase that no quotes can cure) wrote for Hugh in the latter's Album of Asylums and Jails (a kind of diary he kept in those dreadful years):

It is generally assumed that if man were to establish the fact of survival after death, he would also solve, or be on the way to solving, the riddle of Being. Alas, the two problems do not necessarily overlap or blend.

We shall close the subject on this bizarre note.

25

What had you expected of your pilgrimage, Person? A mere mirror rerun of hoary torments? Sympathy from an old stone? Enforced re-creation of irrecoverable trivia? A search for lost time in an utterly distinct sense from Goodgrief's dreadful *'Je me souviens, je me souviens de la maison où je suis né'* or, indeed, Proust's quest? He had never experienced here (save once at the end of his last ascent) anything but boredom and bitterness. Something else had made him revisit dreary drab Witt.

Not a belief in ghosts. Who would care to haunt half-remembered lumps of matter (he did not know that Jacques lay buried under six feet of snow in Chute, Colorado), uncertain itineraries, a club hut which some spell prevented him from reaching and whose name anyway had got hopelessly mixed with 'Draconite', a stimulant no longer in production but still advertised on fences and even cliff walls. Yet something connected with spectral visitations had impelled him to come all the way from another continent. Let us make this a little clearer.

Practically all the dreams in which she had appeared to him after her death had been staged not in the settings of an American winter but in those of Swiss mountains and Italian lakes. He had not even found the spot in the woods where a gay band of little hikers had interrupted an unforgettable kiss. The desideratum was a moment of contact with her essential image in exactly remembered surroundings.

Upon returning to the Ascot Hotel he devoured an apple,

pulled off his clay-smeared boots with a snarl of rejection, and, ignoring his sores and dampish socks, changed to the comfort of his town shoes. Back now to the torturing task!

Thinking that some small visual jog might make him recall the number of the room that he had occupied eight years ago, he walked the whole length of the third-floor corridor – and after getting only blank stares from one number after another, halted: the expedient had worked. He saw a very black 313 on a very white door and recalled instantly how he had told Armande (who had promised to visit him and did not wish to be announced): 'Mnemonically it should be imagined as three little figures in profile, a prisoner passing by with one guard in front of him and another behind.' Armande had rejoined that this was too fanciful for her, and that she would simply write it down in the little agenda she kept in her bag.

A dog yapped on the inner side of the door: the mark, he told himself, of substantial occupancy. Nevertheless, he carried away a feeling of satisfaction, the sense of having recovered an important morsel of that particular past.

Next, he proceeded downstairs and asked the fair receptionist to ring up the hotel in Stresa and find out if they could let him have for a couple of days the room where Mr and Mrs Hugh Person had stayed eight years ago. Its name, he said, sounded like 'Beau Romeo'. She repeated it in its correct form but said it might take a few minutes. He would wait in the lounge.

There were only two people there, a woman eating a snack in a far corner (the restaurant was unavailable, not yet having been cleaned after a farcical fight) and a Swiss businessman flipping through an ancient number of an American magazine (which had actually been left there by Hugh eight years ago, but this line of life nobody followed up). A table next to the Swiss gentleman was littered with hotel pamphlets and fairly recent periodicals. His elbow

98

rested on the *Transatlantic*. Hugh tugged at the magazine and the Swiss gentleman fairly sprang up in his chair. Apologies and counter-apologies blossomed into conversation. Monsieur Wilde's English resembled in many ways that of Armande, both in grammar and intonation. He had been shocked beyond measure by an article in Hugh's *Transatlantic* (borrowing it for a moment, wetting his thumb, finding the place, and slapping the page with the back of his fingers as he returned the thing opened on the offensive article).

'One talks here of a man who murdered his spouse eight years ago and –'

The receptionist, whose desk and bust he could distinguish in miniature from where he sat, was signaling to him from afar. She burst out of her enclosure and advanced toward him:

'One does not reply,' she said, 'do you want me to keep trying?'

'Yes, oh yes,' said Hugh, getting up, bumping into somebody (the woman who had enveloped the fat that remained of her ham in a paper napkin and was leaving the lounge). 'Yes. Oh, excuse me. Yes, by all means. Do call Information or something.'

Well, that murderer had been given life eight years ago (Person was given it, in an older sense, eight years ago, too, but squandered, squandered all of it in a sick dream!), and now, suddenly, he was set free, because, you see, he had been an exemplary prisoner and had even taught his cellmates such things as chess, Esperanto (he was a confirmed Esperantist), the best way to make pumpkin pie (he was also a pastry cook by trade), the signs of the zodiac, gin rummy, et cetera, et cetera. For some people, alas, a gal is nothing but a unit of acceleration used in geodesy.

It was appalling, continued the Swiss gentleman, using an expression Armande had got from Julia (now Lady X), really appalling how crime was pampered nowadays. Only today a temperamental waiter who had been accused of stealing a case of the hotel's Dôle (which Monsieur Wilde did not recommend, between parentheses) punched the maître d'hôtel in the eye, black-buttering it gravely. Did his interlocutor suppose that the hotel called the police? No, mister, they did not. *Eh bien*, on a higher (or lower) level the situation is similar. Had the bilinguist ever considered the problem of prisons?

Oh, he had. He himself had been jailed, hospitalized, jailed again, tried twice for throttling an American girl (now Lady X): 'At one stage I had a monstrous cellmate – during a whole year. If I were a poet (but I'm only a proof-reader) I would describe to you the celestial nature of soli-tary confinement, the bliss of an immaculate toilet, the lib-erty of thought in the ideal jail. The purpose of prisons' (smiling at Monsieur Wilde who was looking at his watch and not seeing much anyway) 'is certainly not to cure a killer, nor is it only to punish him (how can one punish a man who has everything with him, within him, around him?). Their *only* purpose, a pedestrian purpose but the only logical one, is to prevent a killer from killing again. Rehabilitation? Parole? A myth, a joke. Brutes cannot be corrected. Petty thieves are not worth correcting (in their case punishment suffices). Nowadays, certain deplorable trends are current in *soi-disant* liberal circles. To put it concisely a killer who sees himself as a victim is not only a murderer but a moron.'

'I think I must go,' said poor stolid Wilde.

'Mental hospitals, wards, asylums, all that is also fam-iliar to me. To live in a ward in a heap with thirty or so incoherent idiots is hell. I faked violence in order to get a solitary cell or to be locked up in the damned hospital's security wing, ineffable paradise for *this* kind of patient. My only chance to remain sane was by appearing subnormal.

The way was thorny. A handsome and hefty nurse liked to hit me one forehand slap sandwiched between two backhand ones – and I returned to blessed solitude. I should add that every time my case came up, the prison psychiatrist testified that I refused to discuss what he called in his professional jargon "conjugal sex". I am sadly happy to say, sadly proud, too, that neither the guards (some of them humane and witty) nor the Freudian inquisitors (all of them fools or frauds) broke or otherwise changed the sad person I am.'

Monsieur Wilde, taking him for a drunk or madman, had lumbered away. The pretty receptionist (flesh is flesh, the red sting is *l'aiguillon rouge*, and my love would not mind) had begun to signal again. He got up and walked to her desk. The Stresa hotel was undergoing repairs after a fire. *Mais* (pretty index erect) –

All his life, we are glad to note, our Person had experienced the curious sensation (known to three famous theologians and two minor poets) of there existing behind him – at his shoulder, as it were – a larger, incredibly wiser, calmer and stronger stranger, morally better than he. This was, in fact, his main 'umbral companion' (a clownish critic had taken R. to task for that epithet) and had he been without that transparent shadow, we would not have bothered to speak about our dear Person. During the short stretch between his chair in the lounge and the girl's adorable neck, plump lips, long eyelashes, veiled charms, Person was conscious of something or somebody warning him that he should leave Witt there and then for Verona, Florence, Rome, Taormina, if Stresa was out. He did not heed his shadow, and fundamentally he may have been right. We thought that he had in him a few years of animal pleasure; we were ready to waft that girl into his bed, but after all it was for him to decide, for him to die, if he wished.

Mais! (a jot stronger than 'but' or even 'however') she had some good news for him. He had wanted to move to Floor Three, hadn't he? He could do so tonight. The lady with the little dog was leaving before dinner. It was a history rather amusing. It appeared that her husband looked after dogs when their masters had to absent themselves. The lady, when she voyaged herself, generally took with her a small animal, choosing from among those that were most melancholic. This morning her husband telephoned that the owner had returned earlier from his trip and was reclaiming his pet with great cries.

The hotel restaurant, a rather dismal place furnished in a rustic style, was far from full, but one expected two large families on the next day, and there was to be, or would have been (the folds of tenses are badly disarranged in regard to the building under examination) quite a nice little stream of Germans in the second, and cheaper, half of August. A new homely girl in a folklore costume revealing a lot of creamy bosom had replaced the younger of the two waiters, and a black patch masked the grim captain's left eye. Our Person was to be moved to room 313 right after dinner; he celebrated the coming event by drinking his sensible fill – a Bloody Ivan (vodka and tomato juice) before the pea soup, a bottle of Rhine with the pork (disguised as 'veal cutlets'), and a double marc with his coffee. Monsieur Wilde looked the other way as the dotty, or drugged, American passed by his table.

The room was exactly as he wanted it or had wanted it (tangled tenses again!) for her visit. The bed in its southwestern corner stood neatly caparisoned, and the maid who would or might knock in a little while to open it was not or would not be let in – if ins and outs, doors and beds still endured. On the bedside table a new package of cigarettes and a traveling clock had for neighbor a nicely wrapped box containing the green figurine of a girl skier which shone through the double kix. The little bedside rug, a glorified towel of the same pale blue as the bedspread, was still tucked under the night table, but since she refused in advance (capricious! prim!) to stay until dawn, she would not see, she would never see, the little rug doing its duty to receive the first square of sun and the first touch of Hugh's sticking-plastered toes. A bunch of bellflowers and blue-bonnets (their different shades having a lovers' quarrel) had been placed, either by the assistant manager, who respected sentiment, or by Person himself, in a vase on the commode next to Person's shed tie, which was of a third shade of blue but of another material (sericanette). A mess of sprouts and mashed potatoes, colorfully mixed with pinkish meat, could be discerned, if properly focused, performing hand-over-fist evolutions in Person's entrails, and one could also make out in that landscape of serpents and caves two or three apple seeds, humble travelers from an earlier meal. His heart was tear-shaped, and undersized for such a big chap.

Returning to the correct level, we see Person's black raincoat on a hook and his charcoal-gray suitcoat over the back of a chair. Under the dwarf writing desk, full of useless drawers, in the northeastern corner of the lamp-lit room, the bottom of the wastepaper basket, recently emptied by the valet, retains a smudge of grease and a shred of paper napkin. The little spitz dog is asleep on the back seat of an Amilcar driven by the kennelman's wife back to Trux.

Person visited the bathroom, emptied his bladder, and thought of taking a shower, but she could come any moment now – if she came at all! He pulled on his smart turtleneck, and found a last antacid tablet in a remembered but not immediately located coat pocket (it is curious what difficulty some people have in distinguishing at one glance the right side from the left in a chaired jacket). She always said that real men had to be impeccably dressed, yet ought not to bathe too often. A male whiff from the *gousset* could, she said, be most attractive in certain confrontations, and only ladies and chambermaids should use deodorants. Never in his life had he waited for anybody or anything with such excitement. His brow was moist, he had the shakes, the corridor was long and silent, the few occupants of the hotel were mostly downstairs, in the lounge, chatting or playing cards, or just happily balancing on the soft brink of sleep. He bared the bed and rested his head on the pillow while the heels of his shoes were still in communication with the floor. Novices love to watch such fascinating trifles as the shallow hollow in a pillow as seen through a person's forehead, frontal bone, rippling brain, occipital bone, the back of the head, and its black hair. In the beginning of our always entrancing, sometimes terrifying, new being that kind of innocent curiosity (a child playing with wriggly refractions in brook water, an African nun in an arctic convent touching with delight the fragile clock of her first dandelion) is not unusual, especially if a person and the shadows of related matter are being followed from youth to death. Person, *this* person, was on the imagined brink of imagined bliss when Armande's footfalls approached – striking out both 'imagined' in the proof's margin (never too wide for corrections and queries!). This is where the orgasm of art courses through the whole spine with incomparably more force than sexual ecstasy or metaphysical panic.

At this moment of her now indelible dawning through the limpid door of his room he felt the elation a tourist feels, when taking off and – to use a neo-Homeric metaphor – the earth slants and then regains its horizontal position, and practically in no spacetime we are thousands of feet above land, and the clouds (fleecy light clouds, very white, more or less widely separated) seem to lie on a flat sheet of glass in a celestial laboratory and, through this glass, far below it, bits of gingerbread earth show, a scarred hillside, a round indigo lake, the dark green of pine woods, the incrustations of villages. Here comes the air hostess bringing bright drinks, and she is Armande who has just accepted

105

his offer of marriage though he warned her that she overestimated a lot of things, the pleasures of parties in New York, the importance of his job, a future inheritance, his uncle's stationery business, the mountains of Vermont – and now the airplane explodes with a roar and a retching cough.

Coughing, our Person sat up in asphyxiating darkness and groped for the light, but the click of the lamp was as ineffective as the attempt to move a paralyzed limb. Because the bed in his fourth-floor room had been in another, northern position, he now made for the door and flung it open instead of trying to escape, as he thought he could, through the window which stood ajar and banged wider as soon as a fatal draft carried in the smoke from the corridor.

The fire, fed first by oil-soaked rags planted in the basement and then helped up by lighter fluid judiciously sprayed here and there on stairs and walls, swept up rapidly through the hotel – although 'fortunately', as the local paper was to put it next morning, 'only a few people perished because only a few rooms happened to be occupied'.

Now flames were mounting the stairs, in pairs, in trios, in redskin file, hand in hand, tongue after tongue, conversing and humming happily. It was not, though, the heat of their flicker, but the acrid dark smoke that caused Person to retreat back into the room; excuse me, said a polite flamelet holding open the door he was vainly trying to close. The window banged with such force that its panes broke into a torrent of rubies, and he realized before choking to death that a storm outside was aiding the inside fire. At last, suffocation made him try to get out by climbing out and down, but there were no ledges or balconies on that side of the roaring house. As he reached the window a long lavender-tipped flame danced up to stop him with a graceful gesture of its gloved hand. Crumbling partitions of plaster and wood allowed human cries to reach him, and one of his last wrong ideas was that those were the shouts of people anxious to help him, and not the howls of fellow men. Rings of blurred colors circled around him, reminding him briefly of a childhood picture in a frightening book about triumphant vegetables whirling faster and faster around a nightshirted boy trying desperately to awake from the iridescent dizziness of dream life. Its ultimate vision was the incandescence of a book or a box grown completely transparent and hollow. This is, I believe, *it*: not the crude anguish of physical death but the incomparable pangs of the mysterious mental maneuver needed to pass from one state of being to another.

Easy, you know, does it, son.

FOR THE BEST IN PAPERBACKS, LOOK FOR THE 🐧

In every corner of the world, on every subject under the sun, Penguin represents quality and variety – the very best in publishing today.

For complete information about books available from Penguin – including Puffins, Penguin Classics and Arkana – and how to order them, write to us at the appropriate address below. Please note that for copyright reasons the selection of books varies from country to country.

In the United Kingdom: Please write to *Dept E.P., Penguin Books Ltd, Harmondsworth, Middlesex, UB7 0DA.*

If you have any difficulty in obtaining a title, please send your order with the correct money, plus ten per cent for postage and packaging, to *PO Box No 11, West Drayton, Middlesex*

In the United States: Please write to *Dept BA, Penguin, 299 Murray Hill Parkway, East Rutherford, New Jersey 07073*

In Canada: Please write to *Penguin Books Canada Ltd, 2801 John Street, Markham, Ontario L3R 1B4*

In Australia: Please write to the *Marketing Department, Penguin Books Australia Ltd, P.O. Box 257, Ringwood, Victoria 3134*

In New Zealand: Please write to the *Marketing Department, Penguin Books (NZ) Ltd, Private Bag, Takapuna, Auckland 9*

In India: Please write to *Penguin Overseas Ltd, 706 Eros Apartments, 56 Nehru Place, New Delhi, 110019*

In the Netherlands: Please write to *Penguin Books Netherlands B.V., Postbus 195, NL–1380AD Weesp*

In West Germany: Please write to *Penguin Books Ltd, Friedrichstrasse 10–12, D–6000 Frankfurt/Main 1*

In Spain: Please write to *Longman Penguin España, Calle San Nicolas 15, E–28013 Madrid*

In Italy: Please write to *Penguin Italia s.r.l., Via Como 4, I-20096 Pioltello (Milano)*

In France: Please write to *Penguin Books Ltd, 39 Rue de Montmorency, F-75003 Paris*

In Japan: Please write to *Longman Penguin Japan Co Ltd, Yamaguchi Building, 2–12–9 Kanda Jimbocho, Chiyoda-Ku, Tokyo 101*

BY THE SAME AUTHOR

'The variety, force and richness of Nabokov's perceptions have not even the palest rival in modern fiction. To read him in full flight is ... the nearest thing to pure sensual pleasure that prose can offer' – Martin Amis in the *New Statesman*

Laughter in the Dark

A well-nigh medieval cruelty inspires this story of a rich, respectable and happy man whose life ended in disaster.

Pnin

'He can move you to laughter in the way the masters can – to laughter that is near to tears. In Timofy Pnin he has created a character that lives and that sticks in the memory' – *Guardian*

Lolita

'Lolita is not about sex, but about love. Almost every page sets forth some explicit emotion or some overt erotic action and it is still not about sex. It is about love ... it is one of the few examples of rapture in modern writing!' – Lionel Trilling

also published

A Russian Beauty
Ada
Bend Sinister
Despair
Glory
Invitation to a Beheading
Look at the Harlequins!
Mary
Nabokov's Dozen
Pale Fire
Speak, Memory: an Autobiography
The Gift
Tyrants Destroyed

CLASSICS OF THE TWENTIETH CENTURY

The Outsider Albert Camus

Meursault leads an apparently unremarkable bachelor life in Algiers, until his involvement in a violent incident calls into question the fundamental values of society. 'The protagonist of *The Outsider* is undoubtedly the best achieved of all the central figures of the existential novel' – *Listener*

Dark as the Grave wherein my Friend is Laid Malcolm Lowry

A Dantesque descent into hell: into Lowry's infernal landscape of Mexico – the Mexico of his masterpiece, *Under the Volcano* – and into Lowry's own personal abyss, reverberating with mental terrors and spiritual chasms.

I'm Dying Laughing Christina Stead

A dazzling novel set in the 1930s and 1940s when fashionable Hollywood Marxism was under threat from the savage repression of McCarthyism. 'The Cassandra of the modern novel in English … reading her seems like plunging into the mess of life itself' – Angela Carter

The Desert of Love François Mauriac

Two men, father and son, share a passion for the same woman – attractive, intelligent and proud, but an outcast from respectable society because of her position as a 'kept woman'. 'He writes with an intense, almost tempestuous force about the life of the emotions' – Olivia Manning

The Expelled and Other Novellas Samuel Beckett

Rich in verbal and situational humour, these four stories offer the reader a fascinating insight into Beckett's preoccupation with the helpless individual consciousness, a preoccupation which has remained constant throughout his work.

Chance Acquaintances and Julie de Carneilhan Colette

Two contrasting works in one volume. Colette's last full-length novel, *Julie de Carneilhan* was 'as close a reckoning with the elements of her second marriage as she ever allowed herself'. In *Chance Acquaintances*, Colette visits a health resort, accompanied only by her cat.